ONE NIGHT
IN THE ORIENT

ONE NIGHT IN THE ORIENT

BY

ROBYN DONALD

First published in Great Britain 2011
by Mills & Boon, an imprint of Harlequin (UK) Limited.
Large Print edition 2012
Harlequin (UK) Limited, Eton House,
18-24 Paradise Road, Richmond, Surrey TW9 1SR

© Robyn Donald 2011

ISBN: 978 0 263 22544 0

Printed and bound in Great Britain
by CPI Antony Rowe, Chippenham, Wiltshire

CHAPTER ONE

LIFTING a glass of excellent French champagne, Siena Blake said, "Mum and Dad—here's to your next thirty years together! May they be even happier than the ones you've already had."

Diane Blake smiled, serenely elegant in the unfamiliar surroundings of an extremely upmarket London hotel. "Darling, if they're only half as good as the past thirty years they'll be wonderful."

Siena's father gave his wife a look that combined pride and love.

"They'll be better," he said confidently, "and one reason for that is our great good luck with our children. So I'll return the toast—here's to our twins, Siena and Gemma, for making our lives much fuller and more interesting."

He raised his glass, adding slyly, "Although at

our advanced ages I suppose we're now expected to be eagerly waiting for grandchildren."

Sparks flashed from the diamond in Siena's engagement ring as candlelight danced across her taut fingers.

Her voice rang a little false in her ears when she said, "Well, I shouldn't think Gemma has any maternal ambitions. She hasn't yet found a man she'd like to marry, and you'd better give Adrian and me a few years yet." Ignoring a nagging, unwelcome doubt, she took a sip of champagne and set her glass down. "Anyway, the important occasion right now is your anniversary."

A little wistfully her mother said, "The only thing that would be more perfect is if Gemma could have been here too." She smiled. "But she can't, and your arrival yesterday was such a wonderful surprise. I'm only sorry Adrian couldn't make it with you."

Siena thrust aside her strange ambivalence. "He sends his love and best wishes, but he just couldn't take time off work."

Her parents understood. Together they'd built

a business from nothing to a modest prosperity, and with their daughters had lived through times of hard work and sacrifices.

Swiftly Siena added, "Anyway, in a few weeks you'll be home again in New Zealand, and we can celebrate again with Gemma and Adrian and all your friends." She lifted her glass again. "So here's to safe journeys. And a truly fantastic cruise for you both."

As long as she could remember her parents had dreamed of cruising—of taking a leisurely trip through the Caribbean Sea and central America. After years of saving they'd finally set out on a round-the-world odyssey, first touring the United Kingdom before flying out early the next morning to join their ship.

A subdued flurry at the entrance caught her attention. Looking past her mother, she noted with hidden amusement the stately *maître d'hotel* increase pace perceptibly as he made his way across the room to greet some newcomers.

Clearly *important* newcomers. He'd barely acknowledged Siena when she'd arrived to join her parents.

At the unexpected sight of the man who'd just walked in, Siena's heart performed a swift jig in her chest. Setting down her glass with a sharp little movement, she asked abruptly, "Is Nick here to celebrate with us?"

Her parents' surprised looks told her he wasn't. Diane said, "Our Nick?"

"Nicholas Grenville," Siena said, the sound of his name on her tongue tinged with bitterness and shame.

Flinching at her mother's surprised look, she composed her face and disciplined her voice into a steadiness she was far from feeling. "He's just walked in with a stunning woman."

Without turning, Diane asked, "An ash-blonde? Tall, coolly exquisite, superbly dressed?"

"That certainly sounds like the same person." Although all Nick's lovers had been blonde, coolly exquisite, sophisticated, et cetera.

All except one…

Banishing that extremely unwanted thought,

she said hastily, "You know, it seems so unfair I should be barely five foot four inches high when everyone else in our immediate family is tall and elegant."

Even Nick. Unconsciously her gaze flicked across the room as Nick and his partner were shown into an area hidden from most of the diners by a screen of greenery.

Of all the unwelcome coincidences! At least he hadn't seen them.

Smiling, her voice teasing, she said, "Are you sure the nurses in the maternity unit didn't confuse me with another baby?"

Her parents laughed. "Positive," Diane said comfortably. "Apparently you're very like your father's grandmother, who died young. According to family lore she was little and practical and sensible and very forthright. And she had your black curls and those stunning blue eyes."

"I'm glad you still think of Nick as part of our family," Hugh said thoughtfully.

Siena shrugged airily, and bent the truth. "Oh, well, while you were mentoring him Gemma and

I saw him at least once a week for years and years, and every holiday while his mother was working. We thought he was wonderful. He was always lovely to us, although he obviously hadn't had much to do with small girls."

She'd managed not to look across the room again, but she couldn't help asking, "Who is his—the woman with him?"

His latest lover, she thought, a raw edge of old pain surfacing unexpectedly.

Diane exchanged a cryptic glance with her husband. "Portia Makepeace-Singleton. We had dinner in his apartment the night after we arrived in London, and she appeared at his door halfway through the meal. Unexpectedly, I'd say, although you know Nicholas—he gave nothing away."

"I presume she's his latest significant other," Siena said, hoping she sounded coolly dismissive.

Her mother shrugged. "Possibly. Naturally we didn't ask."

Siena looked from one parent to the other. "You didn't like her," she guessed.

Diane looked a little self-conscious and didn't answer directly. "Have they seen us?"

"No, they've been seated out of sight of us less distinguished diners."

But the evening was comparatively young—plenty of time to be noticed, and Nick always noticed.

She wouldn't let Nick's arrival spoil the evening. Defiantly she raised her glass, only to set it down when light scintillated again from Adrian's diamond.

Adrian was a darling. She was very happily looking forward to marrying him next year. He would never hurt her.

Whereas Nick…

She drew in a sharp breath. Nick had almost shattered her.

At sixteen she'd successfully exorcised a crush on her father's protégé. Even then she'd known that Nick was not for her. By the time she'd left high school he'd well outstripped his mentor, made his first millions, and based himself overseas for several years.

He'd stayed in contact with Hugh, sending cards on important dates, calling in to see the family on his visits to New Zealand.

Then, when she'd been nineteen, he'd returned to New Zealand for a few months.

And Siena had been forced to realise she'd been fooling herself. Far from being exorcised, that adolescent crush had metamorphosed into full-blown desire. Oh, she'd fought it, until he'd…

"Siena?"

Jolted back into the present by her mother's puzzled voice, she lifted her glass again and drank a little too deeply of the champagne.

"Sorry," she said automatically. "I was day-dreaming, I'm afraid. I'm overwhelmed by all this glitter and luxury. I wonder what it would be like to live like this?"

Hugh surveyed her with indulgent amusement. "It wouldn't be long before you'd be bored out of your mind. Why don't you ask Nick some day? It's his milieu now that he's a permanent figure in the world's financial pages."

"And described variously—depending on the

journalist—as a buccaneer, a financial genius and an arrogant billionaire far too handsome for his own good," Siena commented, hoping her parents didn't notice the astringent note in her words.

"All accurate," her father said, his tone not entirely approving.

He didn't mention the gossip magazines, with their avid comments on Nick's various relationships. Allowing for the usual frenetic exaggeration, there had been several of those.

Siena wished fervently Nick hadn't come in.

Five years had gone by since she'd seen him last—she'd grown up from the naïve nineteen-year-old she'd been then, abandoning her adolescent fantasies of the perfect hero to settle for a happy future with a lovely man.

It was stupid to be so affected by his arrival.

Not that she'd been the only woman in the room to notice him. His arrogantly handsome features and leanly muscled height gave him a potent charisma that had caught the eye of most of the women in the restaurant.

A very dangerous charisma.

Don't go there...

His presence added to a nameless unease that had been gathering in her for several weeks, a sense that her world—her life—was heading into a grey blandness.

Well, she was probably entitled to a certain concern about her future—a week ago she'd walked out of a perfectly good job.

And now was not the time to be thinking of that disaster. She set her jaw and pushed everything from her mind but the need to enjoy this evening with her parents.

To her relief, a band struck up the sort of music her parents loved. They'd met at a high school ball, and their shared love of dancing was the reason they'd chosen to celebrate their anniversary at this hotel, famous for its dinner dances.

Siena looked at her parents. "What are you waiting for? Up you get."

"Nonsense," her mother said robustly. "We're not leaving you by yourself."

"Mum, of course you must get up. I'm twenty-four! Sitting alone in a restaurant for a few minutes is not going to embarrass me. And I'd like very much to see you dance on your thirtieth wedding anniversary."

After a little more encouragement her parents rose and made their way to the floor. Siena watched them go with a slightly twisted smile. They looked good together, moving with inbuilt, confident grace. Like them, her sister Gemma had hair and skin touched by gold and their long-boned, willowy stature, perfect for a model.

The sort of woman Nick favoured...

Oh, stop it! she commanded. OK, so her unfashionably curly tresses were black, and her skin so pale she didn't dare spend more than a few minutes in New Zealand's notorious summer sun unless she was slathered in sunscreen.

But she had inherited her parents' love of dancing. Smiling, she realised one foot was tapping unconsciously. Using her savings to fly twelve thousand miles as a surprise had been an inspired decision, even if it had cleaned out her bank account. When she'd knocked on their hotel door the previous day her mother had fought back tears and her father had swallowed.

Siena glanced at a woman dressed with such superb taste she shone like a gem even in that gathering of the rich and the famous. Beside her was a notorious and inordinately handsome actor.

The skin between her shoulder-blades tightened. Refusing to turn, she kept her eyes on the dance floor while an odd, primitive apprehension throbbed through her.

From behind her a deep male voice said, "Five years ago you'd have turned to see who was watching you."

Nick.

Deep within her something fierce and bewildering leapt into existence. No, was reborn…

Disconcerted, she focused on the diamond Adrian had given her, and squelched the automatic urge to swivel around. "Five years is a long time, Nick."

Only then did she brace herself and turn to look up into his lean, handsome face. His brows lifted, one slightly higher than the other, as her wary gaze clashed with the hard, dense green of his eyes, exactly the burnished, many-layered colour of *pounamu*, the greenstone prized by both ancient Maori and modern New Zealanders.

Beautiful eyes, she'd thought as an adolescent—and far too perceptive, especially when they were half-screened by thick, long lashes. Once she'd been unable to meet his gaze without a secret inner thrill. The same foolish tension sawed at her nerves now.

"But you still know when someone's watching you," Nick drawled.

"Sometimes," she evaded, a shiver scudding the length of her spine. Unbidden, wildly unsettling memories flooded her brain with disturbing, erotic images. Five years previously she'd lived for a few short weeks in a fantasy world, only to have it all crash down on her in a maelstrom of shattered hopes. Since then she'd made sure she hadn't met him again.

"Do sit down, Nick—you make me feel like a hobbit confronted by an elf." Her words came too quickly, almost tumbling out.

Nicholas Grenville was overpowering in *every* way. Superbly tailored evening clothes emphasised powerful shoulders and long legs, the white shirt contrasting with his coppery tan and black hair and those compelling eyes. But what made him stand out in this assembly of well-dressed, sophisticated men was an unconscious air of command, of hard-edged, formidable authority.

He lowered himself into the chair her father had vacated and enquired, "What are you doing in London? Your parents didn't say they were expecting you."

"They weren't," she told him, still struggling for composure. "I surprised them by arriving yesterday out of the blue."

"Are you on holiday?"

"No," she said crisply. "I left my job."

His brows were raised again. For once, she thought, startled by her satisfaction at the thought, she'd surprised him.

"Why? I thought you were happily settled managing some plant shop."

Her parents must have told him, and Nick

would have filed the information away in that computer brain of his.

Furious and alarmed by the swift surge of warmth that thought aroused, she said, "It wasn't only a plant shop; I managed quite a big nursery as well."

"Did you enjoy it?"

"Very much."

Nick leaned back in his chair and surveyed her. Five years had made quite a difference; a slender blue dress skimmed her body, subtly hinting at tantalising curves beneath, and she'd highlighted the incredible blue of her eyes and her silky, translucent skin with a skilful use of cosmetics. She hadn't quite managed to tame her tumble of ebony curls, and the gaze that met his was reserved, but he discerned a familiar hint of challenge in both eyes and attitude.

Ruthlessly he subdued his body's spontaneous and exasperating response. "So why did you leave?"

She hesitated, then lifted her small square chin in a defiant movement he recognised. "The business was sold, and unfortunately the new owner decided I'd be perfect as a nice little bit on the side."

Gripped by cold, uncompromising anger, Nick forced himself to control it. "And were you?"

Lips tightening, she lifted her hand and splayed the fingers to reveal an engagement ring. "Not interested. But it made for a difficult situation, so I left."

Whatever he'd expected, it hadn't been the sight of that ring. His anger mutated into an emotion he didn't recognise, one he refused to face. He should be—he *was*—pleased she'd fallen in love. Presumably with someone who valued her, a man she could trust—unlike the one who'd taken her virginity and then walked out on her.

That ring and all it implied should go some way to easing his guilt.

It didn't.

It took most of his iron self-control to say curtly, "With a handsome redundancy payment, I hope."

"Absolutely." She beamed at him, a smile that had always meant mischief. "I gave it to a charity for abused women. In his name. They were terribly grateful and no doubt will contact him regularly asking for further donations."

Nick's smile showed his teeth. "A nice little revenge—and typical of you. I assume you had a contract?"

"A contract *I* broke."

"For reasons that could have seen your boss up before the employment court," he said uncompromisingly. "What did your fiancé think of that?"

Siena's eyes widened. Adrian had been angry about the situation, but he'd accepted her handling of it. "He was fine." She hoped her voice didn't sound as defensive as she felt.

Apart from a subtle narrowing of those coolly watchful eyes Nick's expression didn't change. "A rather muted response, surely?"

For him it would have been; even as an adolescent he'd been protective towards two small girls.

But Adrian was nothing like Nick. Adrian would never make love to her as though she was the only woman in the world, then leave the next morning without a word of explanation beyond a few curt phrases of apology for getting carried away.

Adrian wouldn't break her heart.

"Not everyone has your killer instinct," she told Nick with a taut smile. "Adrian knows I can deal with my own problems."

Nick leaned back in his chair and let his gaze rest a moment on her ring finger. Siena had to repress a weird instinct to hide it protectively under the table.

Relentlessly he demanded, "So you walked out of a situation you should never have had to face, with nothing more than your wages, then decided to hop on a plane and meet your parents in London?"

She said cheerfully, "You must be a mind-reader."

His smile was sharp, its humour almost mocking. "No, I happen to remember a wilful, determined child with a big heart. What do you intend to do once you get back home?"

"Find another job, of course."

"Just like that?"

"Give me credit for some intelligence," she said coolly. "I have extremely good references, both from my previous employer and the rat who propositioned me. And while I worked there I learnt a lot about landscaping as well."

Nick nodded. "Your mother told me you'd planned the makeover of their garden. You did a good job—it looks superb."

Hiding her pleasure at this, she said, "Gardening's always been fashionable in New Zealand, and Auckland is a great place for it. Almost everything grows there. As well, the recession has produced a huge surge of interest in being as self-sufficient as possible. Think vegetable gardens and home orchards. I'll find a new position—a better one."

"Still the same confident little thing," he said in a tone tinged with irony. "Tiny and bossy and infuriatingly persistent."

His summing up of her character stung. Producing her sunniest smile, she said, "Remind me to get a reference from you—it can only help."

"Any time," he said laconically. "So, having walked out of your job and on a point of principle donated money you should have put in the bank to a charity, it was an entirely logical decision for you to come to England?"

"It's Mum and Dad's thirtieth anniversary," she explained.

He looked surprised. "They didn't mention it when we had dinner together."

"You know my parents."

His arrogant features softened a little. "Yes. They wouldn't have wanted any fuss."

"We were going to have a party at home—just a small one—and then they planned just to fly over for their dream cruise, but they got a really good deal from one of the big travel firms, with a tour of the UK thrown in first. They weren't going to take it, but Gemma wouldn't have been able to make the party—she's in Australia doing a big promotion for a fashion week there—so I persuaded them to go. And then I decided to come across for the actual day."

He nodded. "And how did your fiancé feel about that?"

"Adrian?" She glanced across, met his burnished green gaze and felt a twinge of sensation in the pit of her stomach. Swiftly she said, "He thought it was a brilliant idea."

"Clearly a very accommodating man." Nick's voice was sardonic.

Siena returned crisply, "Adrian comes from a big family in the South Island. He understands family dynamics."

Too late, she remembered that Nick came from a dysfunctional marriage, and flushed, furious with herself. She was so foolishly conscious of him she couldn't even organise her thoughts.

Nick gave her a narrow smile. "And I don't?"

"I wasn't referring to you." She apologised. "I'm sorry—it was a crass comment."

"But entirely correct," he drawled. Once again he glanced down at her ring. "So when is the wedding?"

"We haven't settled on a date yet," she said, "but almost certainly in the spring next year."

He looked curious. "A long time off. Are you living together?"

"No." The heat in her cheeks flared up again. Her thoughtless comment had been returned with interest and cool deliberation.

Nick looked over her shoulder and rose to his feet, his expression well under control.

Expecting her parents, Siena was surprised by the woman who stopped at the table, but only for a second.

As Nick got to his feet she realised this had to be his latest lover.

CHAPTER TWO

ASSAILED by an emotion perilously close to jealousy—no, Siena corrected hastily, *envy*—she took in the newcomer's tall blonde beauty with something like resignation.

"Nicholas," the new arrival said in a modulated voice. "You see, I wasn't away long."

"Portia, this is Siena Blake," he said negligently, and introduced her.

A pale, expert gaze appraised Siena's blue silk. Appraised—and then dismissed it as a chain store irrelevance. A spark of rebellion lifted Siena's chin a fraction.

Nick finished the introductions. "You met Siena's parents a couple of nights ago," he told the newcomer.

The blonde said smoothly, "I remember. Your fellow New Zealanders." Dismissing them too, she gazed down an aristocratic nose at Siena. "So you and your sister are the—" Her brow crinkled a moment before she laughed softly and directed an arch, long-lashed glance at the man beside her. "I think the words Nicholas used were *'the nearest things I have to sisters.'* Is that right, darling?"

"When I was young, yes," Nick said.

Siena stopped herself from casting him a swift look. Although his tone was perfectly pleasant she detected an edge to it she hadn't heard before.

He finished, "However, it's been some time since I thought of either Siena or her twin as sisters."

"And I'm sure neither of them ever thought of you as a brother." Portia's voice had lowered and she smiled at him.

It wasn't exactly a possessive smile, nor an openly desirous one, but there was a proprietorial gleam mixed with the feminine appreciation. And it cut through Siena's composure like a sword.

What's happening to me? she thought worriedly.

Not that she blamed Nick's lover. Several inches taller than the blonde woman, his black head gleaming in the lights, Nick radiated the cool, leashed assurance Siena always associated with him—as though he could take on the world and win.

Which was exactly what he had done—and on his own terms.

He looked at Siena, his eyes hooded. "Both Siena and her sister considered me an intruder."

Lighten up, Siena told herself. It took an effort to produce a soft laugh. "Especially when you tried to teach us chess."

His grin flashed white. "I was endeavouring not to remember that."

"I'm sure you were an excellent teacher," Portia said a little abruptly, as though somehow Siena had cast aspersions on his intelligence.

"Siena beat me," he told her.

"Because you let me," Siena objected.

She recognised the smile he gave her—amused yet tinged with cynicism. "For the first half of the game, yes," he conceded. "After that I was desperately trying to regain ground."

Portia produced a tinkling little laugh. "And was your sister a prodigy too?"

Nick said, "Gemma was definitely not into board games."

He glanced up as Siena's parents returned, their arrival followed by a flurry of congratulations. In answer to a glance from Nick a waiter glided up to take his order for more champagne, and while that lasted they all made conversation.

Eventually he and Portia went back to their table out of sight. Strung tense as taut wire, Siena forced herself to lean back in her chair and look around the room.

"How lovely to see Nick again," Diane said once they were safely out of earshot. "He was such a tightly buttoned boy I used to worry about him, but things have worked out so well for him." She patted her husband fondly on the arm. "Thanks in no small measure to you, Hugh."

"He'd have got there by himself," Hugh said

confidently. "What we did for him, I think, was to show him what a happy household was like."

Surprised, Siena said, "Do you think so? I wouldn't have thought he'd seen enough of us to do that. From what I remember he spent most of his time doing boy things with you."

Hugh shook his head. "Oh, he knew. Nick's always been extremely astute. When his parents' marriage ended his father was awarded custody at first, then somehow his mother regained it. Shortly after that the father died. I thought it was interesting that Nick never spoke of him."

Diane said quietly, "He did—once—to me. In a chilling, very adult way. He told me he'd never allow himself to be like his father. I wondered if his father had beaten him, but he didn't react like a child who feared physical harm."

Siena was horrified. Her comment to Nick about family dynamics couldn't have been more unfortunate. "Do you think he beat Nick's mother?"

"Possibly," Diane said.

Shocked, Siena tried to reconcile this new information with what she knew of Nick. Somehow—by osmosis, perhaps—she'd absorbed knowledge that his family hadn't been a happy one, but her parents had never discussed him and she'd had no idea his childhood had been traumatic.

Had that trauma something to do with the shattering end to their—their *what*? Romance?

Hardly. Although she'd prayed it might become one. Ever hopeful at nineteen, she thought grimly. Not a romance and neither had it been an affair, because that implied something more important than several weeks of flirtation followed by one night together.

One-night stand she refused to accept. It had been—at least on her side—more than that. She'd been so sure she was in love with him.

Interlude, she decided.

Yes, that fitted the situation perfectly—reduced it to insignificance.

Her mother broke into her thoughts with an inconsequential remark. "It's time Nick got married. He was—what?—thirty in October?"

"In November," her husband informed her.

It figured, Siena thought—Scorpio to the core, she'd bet. Dark and dominant, controlling a passionate nature with a will of steel. Her skin tingled as she remembered…

Diane paused before saying, "I hope Portia isn't what he has in mind."

Siena could only agree. The woman seemed cold—cold to the core.

However, she said lightly, "I'm sure you can leave it to Nick to choose the right woman for him. Now, are you two going to dance again?"

"I'm not—not right now, anyway. But you are," her mother said briskly. "I'm going to repair my lipstick in the wonderful cloakroom they have here, so you two can enjoy this one."

The evening progressed very pleasantly; carefully keeping her gaze well away from the foliage that hid Nick and his lover, Siena watched her parents take the floor. She danced with her father again, and her parents told her all about their short tour.

She despised herself for noticing that Nick and his Portia didn't dance.

Eventually Hugh noticed her hide a yawn. "You must be jet-lagged. I wish you could have found a room in this hotel."

"Dad, I couldn't afford to sleep in the boot cupboard here. I'm so glad you decided to splurge all the way with this trip."

Her parents laughed. "This is the only night we're spending here," Diane admitted.

Siena said easily, "Enjoy it! My hotel might not be anywhere near as opulent as this, but it's perfectly comfortable." She got to her feet and gave her father a quick hug. "I'm only going to be there tonight and tomorrow night—I'm staying in Cornwall with Louise until the end of the week, and then I'm heading home."

"Such extravagance," her mother said fondly, hugged in her turn. "But it was so lovely to see you—a wonderful surprise! I just wish you could come with us on this cruise."

"Don't be silly—you don't want anyone else on your second honeymoon." Siena grinned. As yet her parents didn't know she'd thrown in her job, and by the time they got back she fully intended to have a new position. "Enjoy it to the full, and I'll see you in a month!"

"I'll come down and see you into a taxi," her father stated firmly.

Siena hid a smile. Like Nick, her father was innately protective, and she wasn't surprised when her mother immediately decided to accompany them.

Unfortunately Nick and his girlfriend chose that time to leave, and Nick's offer to take her back to her hotel put her in an awkward position.

"No, thanks, I'll be fine," she said, wondering if the icy chill coming in waves from Portia's direction was real or merely a figment of her too-active imagination. Whatever the other woman had planned for the rest of the evening, it most definitely didn't involve giving Siena a lift anywhere. And Siena definitely didn't want to play gooseberry.

So she said firmly, "Thank you for thinking

of it, but it's not necessary. What on earth could happen to me in a London taxi?"

Nick shrugged. "Where's your hotel?"

When she told him he said, "It's on our way." He nodded at the hotel forecourt. "And there's the car."

He travelled in style. If Portia hadn't been standing frostily by, Siena might have teased him about the large, discreet limousine and uniformed driver that waited for them.

Once she'd have done just that, but Nick now was different from the boy she'd known, the man who had shown her just how intensely wonderful passion could be.

And then left her.

"Nick, dear, that's wonderful of you," her mother interposed. She smiled at Portia. "So kind."

Siena knew when she was beaten. So did Portia, who sketched a thin smile in response.

Fortunately Siena's hotel was a mere five minutes' drive away. She could be polite for that long—and so, she learned, could Nick's lover.

But the atmosphere was not conducive to small talk, and she was glad to get out. "Thanks so much," she said firmly, hoping Nick would take the hint. "Goodnight."

However, he escorted her to the hotel door. "What are you doing after your parents leave?" he asked.

"I'm sightseeing tomorrow, and the next day I'll take the train to Cornwall to stay with an old schoolfriend for a few days," she said, oddly discomposed.

"When did you become engaged?"

The abrupt change of subject startled her into looking up. "Several months ago."

His brows met above the arrogant blade of his nose. "No one told me."

Siena blinked. It sounded like an accusation, but before she could respond, he went on, "Is this Adrian anyone I know?"

"Adrian Worth. His family have a station in the South Island high country." Old money, and a lovely set of relatives. And a very nice, honourable man.

"The name sounds familiar," he said, and left it at that. With a cool smile he nodded and bent his head. Surely he wasn't going to *kiss* her?

He did, a swift peck on her cheek, dropped in place only to be immediately forgotten, she thought, her heart thudding unevenly in her ears when he straightened.

"Sleep well," he said.

Siena couldn't control a startled blink. Nick's narrow smile was *something*. Somehow it roused an excitement she didn't even want to think about. She felt as though she'd been dipped in champagne.

No, she thought cynically, not champagne. The very best brandy—dangerous, delicious and far too potent...

"Goodnight," she managed, and crossed the lobby, feeling the impact of his gaze between her shoulder-blades.

Through the closing lift doors she saw him turn and go back to the big car and the woman who waited for him.

Presumably they'd end the evening in bed together.

Stop being so prying and intrusive, she thought bleakly while the lift eased to a stop. She had no right whatever to speculate about Nick's love affairs.

His private life was just that—private.

Or as private as he could make it with paparazzi following him around.

She spent a restless night, tossing in an unfamiliar bed, listening to traffic, wondering why she wasn't more excited at being in London. Perhaps because at night it was impossible to distinguish between traffic in London and Auckland—a lonely sound in both places.

Eventually she managed to drop off to sleep, only to wake later than she'd planned. A day's sightseeing lay ahead, so she scurried around and left the hotel, intending to grab breakfast and coffee somewhere on her way.

It was a busy day, one she enjoyed. It was only on her way home that she realised she hadn't checked her email. Sitting on the top of the double-decker tourist bus, she flicked her phone open and scrolled through, feeling guilty when she saw one from Adrian.

It took her only a moment to read it, a moment in which the noisy buzz of traffic faded into the sound of her heart drumming in her ears.

I'm so sorry. I'm a complete coward for doing this by email, but I don't know how to tell you I've fallen in love with someone else. It's not your fault, and I feel awful about it, but I can't help it. Please forgive me. You can't think any worse of me than I do myself. I wish you every happiness.

And he was hers sincerely, *Adrian*.

Siena sat in numb, incredulous disbelief, her gaze locked on the screen as Adrian's words danced crazily on it.

An aching emptiness brought a swift, cold spurt of tears. Shivering, she fought them back, trying to tell herself that it was just as well he'd found out now instead of waiting until after they'd married.

Despite the shock, in her innermost heart she knew she'd been waiting for this day. Somehow she'd sensed this—even though she'd refused to face it—long before she'd left New Zealand. For weeks Adrian had seemed distant and on edge, brushing off her enquiries with reassurances that now rang hollow and false.

Nick had called her bossy, and she probably was, but she'd learned to fight for what she wanted. Her parents had always been meticulously fair, but it hadn't been exactly easy growing up in the shadow of a twin who'd been a beautiful baby, progressed to become an enchanting child and then a stunning teenager, before finally maturing into a woman so beautiful she'd dazzled every boyfriend Siena had brought home.

Swallowing hard, Siena fought back nausea. She didn't—refused to—want a man who loved another woman.

So she had to get over this horrible anguish. But first she needed privacy, a few hours alone to deal with her grief. Tomorrow she was heading to Cornwall to stay with her best friend from school, and she would not depress her by moping around.

She clicked off the phone and put it back in her bag, staring resolutely out of the window until she could once more see and hear.

Back at the hotel she fled to her room, eyed the mini-bar, but decided bleakly that a stiff drink was the last thing she needed right now. Opting instead for the familiar solace of a cup of tea, she sat in the uncomfortable chair and forced herself to drink it, trying to achieve some serenity.

None came. Before she'd taken more than a couple of sips she leapt to her feet and, setting her mouth, wrenched off her engagement ring.

No, no longer *her* ring. The diamond winked and glittered in the palm of her hand, and without volition her fingers closed around the lovely thing. She fought back another sob and thrust it into a zipped pocket in her handbag with a sharp, final movement.

Tomorrow it would be on its way back to Adrian.

The hotel telephone rang, making her jump.

Startled, she stared at it, her heart bumping in her chest. It had to be Louise. *Pick it up, Siena!*

But it was Nick's voice that answered her cautious greeting. "Did your parents get off all right?" he said.

"I got a text from Heathrow just before they boarded." Her voice sounded odd.

"What are your plans for tonight?" Nick asked.

"I haven't got any," she said unevenly.

"So you can come out to dinner with me."

She didn't know what to say. "No, that's not possible," she said, obeying the instinct that warned her to hide away for a few hours.

"Why?" he asked.

She stuttered a few words, then stopped.

Into the silence Nick said with a cool decisiveness she found rather intimidating, "There will be just you and me, Siena. I don't like to think of you alone in London."

Say no, it's all right, Nick, I'm fine. But she knew her voice would wobble.

Nevertheless she tried, swallowing first to ease her dry throat, and Nick demanded sharply, "What's the matter?"

"N-nothing." Again her voice betrayed her.

"Siena, I'll be around straight away."

"No!"

But he'd already cut the connection, and after a moment she hung up.

That damned protective instinct, she thought, staring wretchedly down at the half-empty teacup.

She couldn't go out to dinner feeling as though everything that was inside her—heart, passion, laughter and joy—had been scooped out and thrown away, leaving only a shell.

Like Gemma, Nick was accustomed to attention. Even when he'd been a teenager girls had flocked after him, and as he'd grown they'd become more importunate. His meteoric success helped too, she thought with a flash of cynicism.

Once her mother had said with wry amusement, "All it takes is for that green gaze to drift over some woman's face, and she's hooked. It's as though he's a magnet."

Last night almost every woman in the restaurant had given him several intrigued glances, many openly admiring, drawn as much by his leashed, potent energy as his boldly handsome face and that compelling aura that subtly signalled his prowess as a lover.

That thought sent a peculiar shiver down her spine. Ignoring it, she reached for the phone, only to pull back her hand when she realised she didn't know Nick's number. And after minutes of fruitless searching she realised he wasn't listed either. She tried his office, only to be told by some smooth-voiced receptionist that he was unavailable.

Balked, Siena got up wearily and looked out of the window onto the street below. It blurred, and she blinked ferociously to clear an onslaught of tears. Perhaps a shower would clear her head.

She made it short, but when she emerged, fully dressed in case Nick had somehow persuaded the reception clerk to give him a key, her cell phone summoned her.

This time it was Louise.

Ten minutes later Siena put down her cell phone, her friend's strained words still echoing in her ears. "It's my father-in-law," she'd said. "He's had a stroke, and Ivan's mother's at her wits' end with two younger children at home, so we're going up tomorrow. I'm so *sorry*, Siena, but it's impossible for you to stay with us now. But the cottage is here, and we—oh, Siena, I was so looking forward to seeing you…"

Siena had refused the offer of the cottage and done her best to reassure her, but now she stared around the hotel room as though she'd never seen it before.

"What now?" she said aloud, then caught herself up.

No need to feel it was the end of the world. So it had all happened at once, but friends had emergencies and parents went on long-anticipated cruises…

And fiancés fell in love with someone else.

Nobody ever died of a broken heart. Eventually this dull pain would ease.

She dragged in a sharp stabbing breath. She'd organise her return journey to New Zealand, then go down and wait for Nick in the foyer, tell him she couldn't go out to dinner with him.

She would, she thought tautly, be extremely boring company, and he'd probably only asked her because he knew her parents were leaving and she'd be alone.

In effect, he'd behaved just like the brother he considered himself to be.

Nick saw her as soon as he entered the foyer. She hadn't noticed him, and something about the way she was sitting made him frown, and quicken his pace. A friend had once described her—patronisingly—as "a taking little thing". Tiny and black-haired, with eyes so blue they were a startling contrast to her porcelain skin, she certainly looked doll-like—except for her mouth. Lush, sensuously curved, her mouth was a delicious miracle made for smiles—and kisses.

Now it was pinched, and set in a straight line. She was holding herself stiffly, warding off an invisible blow. Nick swore under his breath and increased the length of his stride.

It was impossible to link Siena with the word defeat, but that was how she looked—as though she'd been knocked to the ground so roughly she couldn't be bothered getting up again. And she certainly wasn't dressed for dinner.

Her parents…?

"What's the matter?" he demanded from two strides away.

She blinked as though she didn't recognise him. Then with a brave attempt at her usual spark she said, "Oh, a couple of things, but it's not the end of the world."

Nothing had happened to Hugh and Diane, then. Hiding his relief, he said more moderately, "So tell me."

The hands in her lap tensed. No ring, he realised. What the hell—?

She said, "Well, I think I mentioned I was going to stay with a friend in Cornwall, but that's off."

Nick listened to her explanation, nodding when she finished. "So what are you going to do?"

Her white teeth dented her curved bottom lip. Nick's gut tightened in spontaneous appreciation of that succulent mouth. Damn it, asking her out had been a bad idea; he should never have succumbed to the questionable impulse.

Getting to her feet, she said in a rigidly controlled voice, "I'm trying to get a flight back home."

"And?"

"So far no luck, but I'll keep at it."

Nick frowned. "So you've got a week to spend in London?"

She shook her head. "No."

"Why?"

"Can't afford it," she admitted, lifting her chin to give him a direct glance that glittered a challenge. "I have to go home."

Now was not the time to press her about the absence of her engagement ring. He owed it to her parents to make sure she was all right. "We can discuss your options over dinner. Come on."

After a moment's hesitation she shook her head. "I'd really rather not, Nick. I'm not dressed—"

"It's all right. We'll eat at my place."

He saw her waver and felt an odd, irritating triumph when she nodded.

"Very well," she said quietly, as though too tired to protest further. But once she got up she made a final objection. "Nick, I'm probably not going to be very good company."

"Why?"

"Oh, nothing important." Her voice was stronger, more like the Siena he knew.

You're lying. And you'll tell me what's going on before the evening's out, he thought. The Siena he remembered wouldn't have let a change in plans affect her like this.

She said, "I'll go up and get changed. I won't be any more than ten minutes."

"You're fine the way you are," he told her.

After giving his suit a brief glance she said with a return to her usual tone, "I'll change."

Shoulders held very erect, she walked across the foyer towards the lift. Although small, he thought, his loins stirring again, she was in perfect proportion. Well-worn jeans showed off slim, elegantly shaped legs, and the clear pink thing she wore on top marked every curve of breast and hip, and the narrow allure of her waist.

He wasn't the only one watching her. The receptionist, a boy not long out of his teens, was also following her progress with too much interest. A spurt of anger took Nick by surprise.

He caught the kid's eye, and was coldly and foolishly pleased when he flushed and with a bobbing Adam's apple got busy with the computer. Nick transferred his gaze to two other men. Hastily they abandoned their interested survey and disappeared into the bar.

Satisfied, Nick quelled his cold disapproval and waited.

CHAPTER THREE

SIENA eyed her blue dress—a little tired after its outing the previous night, but it was all she had. Nick had somehow managed to overcome her instinctive need to hide away like a wounded animal—aided by her realisation that she'd be better off in his powerful, formidable presence than sitting alone in her hotel room wondering why her only two serious relationships had ended with the men she loved—or thought she loved—leaving her.

That bitter feeling of alienation chilled her. She struggled with the impulse to tear off her clothes and crawl into bed. It wouldn't work—if she knew one thing about Nick it was that he was determined. One way or another, he'd get her out of her room.

Anyway, self-pity was a loser's indulgence.

But the prospect of eating anything made her feel sick, a nausea that escalated when the lift started to take her down.

When she saw Nick, darkly dominant and looking more than a little grim, she managed a smile. He didn't return it. Head held high, she parried his keen scrutiny and a strange alteration to her heartbeat transmuted into racing pulses and a moment of lightness, of keen anticipation.

"I only brought one going-out-to-dinner outfit," she told him. Heavens, was that her voice—husky and almost hesitant?

Get a grip, she ordered.

"So? You look charming," he said calmly, and took her arm. "I suppose you travelled with nothing more than hand luggage?"

Rills of sensation ran from his fingers to her spine, spreading out through every cell in a gentle flood. Almost she shivered, and it took a considerable amount of self-control to respond in the easy tone of one old friend to another, "Afraid not. I expected to be here for a week, and as it's winter on this side of the equator I had to pack warm clothes. *I* don't have a home in every capital, with wardrobes full of clothes made specially for me."

"Neither do I," he said crisply, nodding to the doorman.

"Just about."

He gave her a saturnine smile. "I own two dwellings."

"Which one do you call home?"

For a moment she thought he wasn't going to answer, but he said finally, "The one in Auckland."

Strangely that warmed her as Nick guided her into the waiting car.

Once inside he turned to her. "Apart from your friend's news, did you have a good day?"

"Most of it was great, thank you." She made him laugh, relating a small incident in a park involving an elderly dowager and a small child, and slowly her tension subsided.

She even thought bracingly, *I can do this. I can stay in one piece long enough to last out the evening.*

Once she got herself onto a plane she could shatter if she needed to. Nobody would know her, so nobody would care if she spent the whole trip in glum silence.

But first she had to get her ticket changed…

Nick said, "I called my PA while you were dressing. There's a possibility of an immediate trip back to New Zealand. She might ring while we're having dinner."

"Oh—Nick, that's kind of you, but you didn't need to." She glanced at his unsmiling face, and ignored a vagrant shiver down her spine when his lashes drooped. "Your poor PA—she's probably muttering oaths under her breath."

"I doubt it. She's paid well, worth every penny, and accustomed to being on call whenever I need her."

Siena imagined a prim, super-efficient middle-aged woman, silently and hopelessly in love with her employer. "At night?" she asked without trying to hide her scepticism. "Obviously she has no family."

"On the contrary, she has two small children."

Nick went on smoothly, "Her husband is the housekeeper in that home."

Siena digested this in silence. "Very modern."

"It works for them. You'd probably like them—they're an interesting couple."

Absently Siena nodded, but said, "Won't she need my ticket number and other information? You should have told me at the hotel and I could have got it for you."

"If she does, tomorrow morning will be soon enough."

By then the car was slowing down in a quiet street flanked on either side by rows of lovely Georgian houses.

Siena gazed through the vehicle window with appreciation. "If anyone had asked me, I'd have said you'd choose an ultra-modern penthouse in a tower block."

"I prefer this."

"Who wouldn't?" She gave a wry smile. "Actually, it suits you—very studied, very controlled." *And gorgeous...* "I can see you as a Regency buck, driving your phaeton and four up to the door."

"I'd have to check, but I suspect phaetons only had two horses," he said.

"Trust you to know that," she said on a half-laugh.

One brow lifted, he looked down at her. "Why?"

"When we first met you Gemma and I decided you knew everything important in the world."

His beautiful mouth quirked. "Six years' difference in age can do that. Growing up must have meant sad disillusion for you both."

He stopped, and for a moment she thought she saw something like regret darken his eyes. Was he remembering that he'd had a hand in shattering more than a few of her illusions?

Probably not. Turning her head so he couldn't see her face, she pretended to examine the street, serene and gracious in the light of the lamps.

Even at nineteen she'd been worldly-wise enough to know that the link between them was fragile and not likely to last. The knowledge hadn't prevented her heartbreak, but at least Nick had never made any promises to her.

She shouldn't have come with him. When she could trust her voice she said steadily, "Disillusion happens to everyone."

"To those who still have illusions," he said, his voice hard and level. "Siena—"

He stopped, his mouth thinning as the car drew up in front of a flight of steps leading to an impressive door.

Right then Siena would have given everything she owned to be somewhere—anywhere—else. The very last thing she wanted from him was an apology for his behaviour five years ago.

Once inside the building she gazed around with undisguised interest and quickly, before he could say any more, said, "Nick, this is lovely."

"I'm glad you think so."

The graceful drawing room was furnished with an aura of elegant restraint that echoed her host's vital, coolly self-disciplined authority. The decorator had married antique and modern pieces with flair and style.

"Whoever did this knew you very well," she said without thinking.

He ignored the comment. "I think you need an aperitif. Still Sauvignon Blanc?"

"Yes, thank you." It had been years since she'd told him how much she enjoyed that particular wine, and she was surprised and strangely cheered that he remembered.

It was a New Zealand white, crisp and delicious, and after the first sip she set the glass down and looked at him. That odd kick in her heartbeat startled her again. "You can take the Kiwi out of New Zealand…" she teased.

His smile was a little narrow. "I like other wines as well, but this seemed appropriate for tonight. Here's to your happiness. Why aren't you wearing your engagement ring?"

Siena flinched, her gaze falling to her empty finger. Adrian hadn't stayed around for long, she thought on a spurt of anger. A thin line of slightly paler skin revealed that she'd been wearing the ring for only a short time.

It was still in her hotel room. When she'd enquired about the cost of sending it back, the insurance had been so much she'd been unable to afford it.

It took a lot of willpower to meet Nick's green eyes, but she parried their unsparing assessment with head held high. She wouldn't lie to him.

Straightening her shoulders, she said briefly, "When I got back to my room in the hotel there was an email from my fiancé telling me he'd found someone else."

The base of Nick's glass made a sharp little clink as he set it down on the nearest table. He strode towards her, his expression formidably angry. "An *email*?" he demanded incredulously.

Clutching her glass, she nodded, unable to articulate her tumbling thoughts.

Nick opened his mouth, then closed it again, biting back words she was glad she didn't have to hear. He took her glass and set it down, then drew her towards him. On an uneven sigh Siena let herself relax into the strong arms enfolding her. Her forehead came to rest on a powerfully muscled shoulder as he stroked slowly across her back in soothing, potently comforting movements.

Siena dragged in several more ragged breaths and abandoned herself to the simple relief of being held.

In a cold, uncompromising voice he said, "Cry if you want to."

"I don't," she said, blinking back ferocious tears. If she cried it would be because Nick was being so kind—in a brotherly way, of course, she reminded herself drearily.

Well, that was all right.

Still in that formidable tone he said, "It's too early to say this, but anyone who would break off an engagement by email is someone you don't need in your life."

And when she stayed silent he added, "Not now and not ever."

She nodded. "I know," she muttered. "It's all right. I'm not going to crack up."

"I didn't expect you to. Not you."

Something melted deep inside her. The warmth of his embrace and the lithe power and strength

of his support—entirely lacking in sensuality—
gave her strength. Her taut muscles loosened,
became freer, her breaths evening out so that the
sobs she dreaded didn't come to fruition.

Slowly—so slowly she had no idea what was
happening—the wave of misery receded. Yet still
she didn't pull away, and Nick didn't drop his
arms.

At first without realising it, she began to respond to the soothing movement of his hand
across her back. Her body stirred, sending secret,
unsuspected signals that blossomed into a tantalising awareness, an insidious pleasure that sang
through her in heady invitation.

A shiver of mixed anticipation and apprehension shocked her into pulling back. Instantly he
released her and stepped away, examining her
with the burnished gaze that successfully hid his
thoughts.

Hot shame rushed through Siena. Rushing
into speech she said, "Thanks." And managed
to sketch a smile. "You should have had sisters—
you make a great brother."

His brows lifted, and the smile he gave in return was sardonic. "Any time you need a fraternal shoulder, just let me know," he said, drawling the words with an intonation that deepened her flush.

"I hope I never do again." Her voice was pitched too high. Avoiding his glance, she picked up her wine glass.

Fine tremors shook her hand, and she hoped he couldn't see the shimmer across the surface of the liquid when she lifted it to her lips. After the smallest of sips she set the glass back down again in case he'd noticed.

But he was looking at his watch. Immediately, as if he'd somehow summoned her, a woman appeared with a tray of small savouries. Nick introduced her as his housekeeper and when she'd gone he ordered, "Have something to eat. You're as pale as a ghost."

Obviously he hadn't felt anything like that heady, sensuous connection. He probably hadn't even realised what his closeness was doing to her.

Thank heavens. "Hadn't you noticed I'm always

pale?" she said crisply. "Although I prefer to think of myself as ethereally fair."

His half-smile told her he knew what she was doing. "Ethereal? Not with devil-black curls and that smart mouth. I have to leave you—I'll be no more than five minutes. When I come back I want to see several of those savouries eaten."

Siena glowered balefully after him as he left the room, but although she wasn't hungry the little mouthfuls of food looked delicious and smelt divine. Almost without thinking, she picked one up and nibbled, trying to sort out her thoughts and her odd reactions.

She was over Nick. Had been for years. She no longer even wanted to know why he'd made love to her with such wild tenderness, then left her with nothing more than an abrupt and angry statement that he'd lost his head and he was sorry.

As well as showing her how passionate she could be, Nick had hurt her—*damaged* her in a way she hadn't understood or recognised until that moment. Unwittingly she must have vowed never to allow herself to feel so intensely again.

It had taken all her will, but she'd eventually managed to put him behind her and get on with her life. She'd met someone safe—someone she'd been sure would never cause her the pain Nick had...

She winced. Was that really why she'd chosen Adrian? Surely her love for him hadn't been a mirage, desperately conjured by memories of the dark sorcerer who'd shown her passion and joy and then abandoned her to a world without either?

If so—if she'd let her misery at Nick's rejection make the choice for her—perhaps Adrian had sensed it...

What weird power did Nick have that just being held in his sexless embrace roused a long-repressed hunger?

OK, so the day had flung a couple of nasty surprises at her—well, one shock and one disappointment—leaving her off-balance, stranded and short of money on the other side of the world from home. She'd been worried, but she'd have managed.

Then Nick had arrived. Being Nick, he'd taken over and…

And what?

In his aloofly controlled way he'd been protective and kind—clearly signalling that he was doing his duty to the couple who'd helped him when he was young and more vulnerable.

The soft sound of the door made her look up sharply. Her stomach dropped as Nick came in, black brows almost meeting across his nose.

"What's the matter?" she asked.

The frown smoothed out. "My question, I think. You look shell-shocked."

"I'm fine," she said automatically.

"And so am I." He examined her face, then said with a touch of irony, "All right, I've just had a conversation with my PA that means I have to rearrange my schedule. It's no big deal."

Without preamble she said, "I used to resent you when I was a kid."

He looked across at her, his brows slightly

raised. "I know. You always wanted to come with us when your father and I went off to the various sports and games he introduced me to."

"I must have been a brat."

"Not exactly that," he said dryly. "You were an uncompromising little thing, and very determined. I got used to thunderous frowns, black looks, pouting—"

"I never pouted!"

"You did, and very cutely. I didn't blame you."

"Generous of you," she said with a wry smile. And because she'd always wondered, she asked, "How did you find yourself being Dad's protégé?"

His expression tightened, but he spoke easily enough. "After my own father died I became hard to handle. My mother was desperate enough to contact an organisation that helped fatherless boys, one your father had volunteered for. We clicked."

He stopped, then went on almost harshly, "I owe him an immense debt. When I decided to go out on my own in IT he couldn't afford to back me financially, but he introduced me to people who could, and he gave me both intellectual and moral support."

Very moved, she said, "That's quite a tribute. But you did something for him too, you know. You were the son he never had."

"I hope so," he said, in a tone that came close to being dismissive, as if he'd said too much. "Dinner's ready now if you are."

Siena had been satisfied by the two small savouries she'd eaten, but the wine was making its effects felt. She felt disconnected, the raw shock of Adrian's rejection lightly blanketed by a buzz in her head that told her she needed food.

Stubbornly she forced herself to eat, but halfway through the main course she stopped, shivering, and the words she'd been trying to get out refused to come. Horrified, she froze.

"You're probably still jet-lagged, and in shock," Nick said abruptly, getting to his feet. "You can stay the night here."

"No, I—"

He interrupted curtly, "You need rest. And

you're in no fit state to be on your own. I'll get a bed made up for you and tomorrow morning we can discuss what you'll do."

"N-Nick, there's no reason…" She said feebly, "I must have had too much wine."

"I doubt if half a glass would have this effect on you," he said, his tone edging towards boredom. "Siena, stop fighting it. You've had a rotten day. A decent sleep should help, but you're not going back to that hotel. I want to make sure you're all right."

It would be so easy to give in to that masterful tone, to let Nick look after her, but she summoned her strength and said again, "No."

"Then I'll contact your parents and tell them you're in trouble," he said.

Siena stiffened, incredulity temporarily swamping her tiredness. "D-don't you d-dare," she stammered. "They've—they've been looking forward to this holiday for years. You wouldn't really do that to them?"

He raised his eyebrows. "Of course I would,"

he said coolly. "It's exactly what they'd expect me to do."

She couldn't dispute that. Rallying, she challenged fiercely, "That would be *betrayal*."

"I fancy they'd think that not telling them would be the greater treachery."

Searching his face, she felt her heart clamp when she saw no gentleness, no sign of compromise in the hard, angular features.

She attempted a laugh, only to find it ignominiously turning into something too close to a sob. "You mean you'll tell on me," she said, backing her caustic tone with the terminology of childhood to make her opinion of his threat clear.

"If you like to look at it that way, yes." Nick waited, and when she stayed silent his eyes narrowed. "So?"

Abruptly she surrendered. "Damn you. All right," she said unevenly.

"Wait here while I sort out a bed for you," he ordered. "And eat something more."

But the food tasted like cardboard, and when

Siena tried to swallow she had to drink water to force it past the lump in her throat.

Nick's return brought her head up. With a snap she said, "I *hate* feeling like this."

He looked grimly amused. "Yes, I imagine you do. But you'll get over it. You have too much energy—too much resilience and willpower—to let life keep you down for long. And sleep is a great healer."

Being Nick, he was probably right, she thought drearily as she slid naked into the bed in one of the guest rooms. But right now she couldn't summon a spark of resilience, or the willpower to shut out the mess she'd somehow managed to make of her life.

When her phone summoned her she ignored it, but it nagged at her until finally she switched on the lamp and picked it up.

It was her sister. Incredulously she read an email, a tumbling apology for something—what?

When she reached the end, she stared incredulously as the tiny screen. Gemma—and *Adrian*?

Gemma had tried to reach her at the hotel by

phone, but there had been no answer. Siena recognised her sister's desperation as she apologised for loving Adrian, saying she'd tried so hard not to—she'd go away, never see him again…

"I *can't*…" Siena didn't finish.

Dry-eyed, she hunched back against the pillows, thoughts tumbling through her mind in chaotic freefall.

But eventually she dragged in a deep, painful breath and straightened up. The habit of caring for her emotional sister was too deeply engrained for her to leave Gemma in such turmoil.

It took her a tense half-hour to formulate some coherent reassurance, and she even managed to state that she was spending the night at Nick's lovely house before signing off.

And then she lay still and rigid in the huge, opulent bed before falling into a mercifully deep sleep.

She dreamed—snatches of scenarios in which she was searching for someone, calling an unknown name as she stumbled through rainforest, impeded by clutching branches that seemed alive and evil. And all the time knowing that if she dared stop something dangerous would seize her and carry her off and she'd never again see the person she sought.

"Siena, wake up!"

Nick's command splintered the dream into shards that disappeared like smoke in the wind. A hard hand on her shoulder shook her into consciousness, and when her eyes sprang open she saw his face, intent and close to hers. Her heart leapt in her chest.

"It's all right," he said, his voice softening a little, "you're just dreaming. It's over now."

She shuddered, and to her horrified shock couldn't hold back the hot tears. Muttering something savage beneath his breath, Nick sat down on the side of the bed and took her in his arms.

He held her as he had before, offering her the silent comfort of his strength and nearness, his presence. She fought back the tears, and as the dream faded she relaxed against the heat and power of his body, surrendering to the security of his heartbeat and his arms around her.

Slowly—so slowly she didn't know exactly when the knowledge finally seeped into her brain—she realised that the male skin she'd wet with her tears was bare.

As she was. From breast to waist they were pressed together, skin against skin, so that she could feel the driving beat of his heart, the heavy thud of it almost as unsteady as hers.

Long-repressed memories surged back—memories of the night they'd spent together, the night Nick had introduced her to passion and taken her virginity.

She hadn't known desire could transform into an elemental force—wild yet tender, sensuous and gentle, and then a whirlwind of untamed sensuality that stripped her of everything but the need to give and take, to join Nick in surrender to the consuming urgency of need.

And do you remember what happened afterwards...?

Valiantly she tried to take refuge in the secure armour of those bitter memories, but her traitor mind stayed fixed on their entwined heartbeats as the muscles of his shoulder tensed and flexed beneath her cheek.

Exultant, terrified, she knew she should pull away.

"I know I told you to cry before," he said in a controlled voice, his voice vibrating inside his chest so that she could feel the words as well as hear them, "but I should have known you'd fling yourself into weeping as energetically as you do everything else."

Siena dragged in a long, hiccupping breath. She was too close, too aware of a faint, evocative fragrance—the drifting vapour of some soap mingled with a darkly sensuous scent that was Nick's alone, a disturbing male summons.

In the pit of her stomach that forbidden sensuousness uncoiled, spreading so swiftly she couldn't contain it. It weakened her so that she didn't want to pull away—no, *couldn't* pull away...

This is Nick, she tried telling herself, but although the words circled through her brain, the drugging effect of being close to Nick remained.

Nick, she thought feverishly, *who left you alone and humiliated...*

Adrian's betrayal had little power over her now.

She looked up, meeting eyes of blazing, intent green. Her own widened, roaming the dark, arrogant features, and that frisson of reckless desire sizzled through her—velvet and fire, honey and spice, summoning a tide of voluptuous heat in every cell.

Nick's eyes narrowed and his lashes drooped. As though he couldn't stop himself, he bent his head and his mouth crushed hers. She stiffened, but almost immediately she gave up thinking, lashes fluttering down in dangerous surrender to his passion.

Until he broke the kiss and said harshly, "I don't do comfort sex, Siena. If you want this, you have to understand who's kissing you, who'll be taking you. And there won't be anything comfortable and friendly about it."

It took a second or two for his meaning to sink in. When it did, shame submerged her in a chilly deluge. Although the last thing she wanted was to see the contempt she heard in his voice, she dragged in a juddering, painful breath and opened her eyes, meeting a burnished, metallic gaze she couldn't read.

"I can't… No, I don't want that," she muttered, and pulled herself away, only to realise that this exposed her bare torso to his gaze.

Nick's hooded gaze didn't waver. Embarrassed, she grabbed at the sheet, but he was sitting on it.

He got up in one lithe movement, turning away so he didn't see how desperately she retreated behind the fragile shield of fabric, so drugged by a bewildering mixture of emotions she couldn't formulate any words that might sound sensible.

He was clad only in a pair of pyjama pants, and the sight of him—big, sleekly bronzed, powerful with a build that could only come from sheer strength—made her mouth go dry.

Siena swallowed, and said thinly, "I'm sorry. I don't…I don't know what came over me."

His smile was sardonic. "It's called proximity, and it's pretty universal. It happened to us once before, remember?"

Oh, God, if only she could forget!

"Yes, I remember." Ignoring the colour that suffused her skin, she met his eyes with dogged determination.

Before she could say anything he went on harshly, "I regret—intensely—my behaviour that night. I wish I'd handled it better so that we could have remained friends."

Proximity? Friends?

The cool lack of emotion in his tone, in his choice of words, hit her like a shower of frigid water. Steadying her voice, she said, "Nick, it's all right. D-don't worry about it. It's over now, in the past."

After a moment's hesitation she went on in a rush, "Gemma emailed me. It's—she and Adrian are in love. She's desperately miserable about the situation."

He gave her a keen look. "So you want to go home and take care of her."

"I want to get home as soon as I can," she said shortly. "I'm sorry for weeping all over you. I haven't had a nightmare since I was a kid."

Before she had time to think, she added with an attempt at lightness, "You needn't be concerned that I'll tell Portia what happened."

"I'm not." He didn't try to temper his curtness. "We don't have that sort of relationship."

So why did she call you darling?

A swift, shaming flare of jealousy consumed her, and she was appalled by an urge to ask him to elaborate on that terse statement. Firming her lips, she held the words back by force of will.

Not that she'd have got an answer. He was already turning away.

Siena's throat closed and her heart jumped in her chest. Even from the back he was stunning. His coppery hide highlighted wide shoulders and narrow hips to perfection, the taut skin smoothing over long, powerful muscles.

Made shy by his dynamic physical perfection, a need she didn't understand compelled her to say his name.

He stopped and half turned to look at her. "What is it?"

She said huskily, "Thank you for your...for

comforting me." And added crossly, "I wish I could finish just one sentence instead of stumbling over words!"

"You just did," he said, smiling briefly. "Do you think you'll be able to sleep now?"

CHAPTER FOUR

SIENA understood. Nick was deliberately turning the clock back, trying to restore their relationship to its previous standing of almost-family. Shocked by the strength of her dismay, she stemmed the protest that trembled on her tongue.

She said quietly, "Yes, of course."

"I'll get you something to drink." His mouth quirked in a familiar mixture of mockery and amusement. "You'll need to rehydrate after all those tears."

"Thank you, but I can get some water for myself." Desperate for him to go, she glanced at the door to the charming small *en suite* bathroom.

"Stay there," he said tersely.

Hurt by the edge to his voice, she tried to suppress the strange jumble of thoughts and emotions churning through her, closing her eyes until he came back.

Not that she'd hear him. He'd always moved silently—a born predator, her father once had called him.

Well, her father had been wrong. If Nick had been a predator then right now—at this very minute, she thought with a voluptuous heat melting her bones—they'd be erotically entwined in the great bed.

Because she had as little resistance to his dangerous charm as when she'd been a virginal nineteen-year-old.

Fortunately—*fortunately*, she emphasised to her wistful heart—he'd had the self-control to stop and make sure she understood his lovemaking would be what it had been then. Nothing more than an emotionless passion—mere animal hunger with no feelings beyond the physical.

He'd given her the chance to pull back.

She had to be glad she'd taken that chance. Surrendering would have been the most foolish thing she'd ever done—apart from yielding to her own importunate desire that long-ago, better-forgotten night.

Nick's voice jolted her lashes upwards. "Most people prefer to sleep lying down. Here, drink this."

"Thank you," she said huskily, fingers gripping the smooth, cool tumbler. Her hand shook, so she hastily lifted it to her mouth and managed to get some of the water down her parched throat without spilling any.

"Sleep well," he said after another of those metallic, unreadable glances. He turned and walked out of the room, the light gleaming golden over his lithe, powerful form.

The chill Siena had felt after the kiss was reinforced by his very definite rejection.

So what was new? She sipped more water and tried to organise her chaotic, bewildered thoughts.

Nick's first instinct had been to comfort. The situation had changed only once she'd calmed down enough to realise what was happening to her. Men could want women they disliked, so it

wasn't surprising he'd responded to her unconscious nestling against him.

But why had she allowed the security of Nick's
arms around her, his rock-solid embrace, to
banish everything else from her mind?

Had her love for Adrian, that gentle, safe refuge
from any chance of anguish, not been love at all?

That was even worse, she thought miserably,
sickened by the possibility of her own self-
deceit. Surely it wasn't true—after all, she'd been
shocked by Adrian's email.

Shocked and upset.

Gemma's email had added to her distress, its
wildly passionate tone a real worry. She needed
to get back home as quickly as she could so she
could convince her sister—and maybe by exten-
sion herself—that Gemma hadn't wrecked her
life.

Hastily she drank more, before setting the tumbler down with a small clink on the bedside table
and closing her eyes again. She had to face the
truth. Her main emotions were astonishment, and
a kind of chagrin, not the fierce, bleak grief that

had gripped her for months when Nick had left New Zealand after their night together.

Yet the wild need that had propelled her into Nick's bed hadn't been love. It was lust.

And now she knew it was powerful enough to rekindle a fire that had lasted five long years. In Nick's arms she'd been utterly blown away by the sensations rioting through her.

Nick hadn't.

Oh, he'd wanted her—but he'd been able to control himself.

She grabbed the tumbler and gulped the last mouthful of water, coughed as it went down the wrong way, and breathed through her nose. Once her spluttering had eased, she found herself thrilling to the memory of that kiss.

Let it go, she told herself fiercely. *You lost your head. It happens. Get over it.*

Now she knew how shamefully susceptible she was to his powerful charisma she'd make sure it didn't happen again—and so, no doubt, would Nick. He wasn't into serious relationships, and right now she'd had enough of them too.

Once she got home, safely distant from Nick's orbit, she'd avoid him as she had these past years. She'd set herself to finding a decent position where her immediate boss was either a woman, or safely and happily married.

The searing intensity of Nick's kiss meant nothing.

So tomorrow she'd have to make it clear she understood—that she wasn't expecting anything from him.

Well after dawn she was woken by the housekeeper carrying a breakfast tray. Clever of Nick, she thought as she thanked the woman. It was a good way to put off the meeting she dreaded. She ate most of the delicious food, drank some restorative coffee, but eventually had to emerge from the bedroom.

As if she'd been lying in wait, the housekeeper instantly appeared. "Mr Grenville would like to see you in his study, miss, if that's all right?"

Siena braced herself. "Can you show me where that is?"

"This way."

Nick's study was more of an office; Siena's swift survey revealed a very impressive communications set-up on a large desk and a set of filing cabinets, their businesslike impact softened by shelves of books and a stunning oil of a place she recognised immediately. The pictured beach was the one that spread out below his house on Auckland's North Shore.

The owner of all this was standing by the window, watching her. Of course he didn't look any different, whereas she felt as though somehow last night—no, she conscientiously amended, the previous twenty-four hours—had begun a fundamental process of change.

And that was a very, very scary thought.

Nick's enigmatic gaze probed her face in an examination that had her stomach twisting—a sensation halfway between apprehension and a shameful thrill until it settled on her dress, and he allowed himself a slight oblique smile.

"I know, I know," she said crisply, determined to sound her usual self. "Very morning-after-the-night-before-ish."

A muscle flicked in his jaw, but when he spoke his tone couldn't have been more neutral. "You look lovely, as always."

"You're thinking of my sister," she corrected, aware that she was not lovely. Good skin, yes. Nice hair, certainly.

Lovely, never.

"Gemma is beautiful," he agreed, "but you've always been extremely attractive. Are you envious of your sister's beauty?"

Surprised by the direct question, she didn't have to think about it. Shaking her head vigorously she said, "No. What I'd really like is her long legs. I think I suffer from small person's syndrome because I've always had to crane just to see what everyone else does."

He laughed out loud at that. "Your legs are in proportion. As for small person's syndrome, I doubt that. Your mother says you were born determined to establish your place in the world."

"Stroppy," she sighed. This was the Nick she'd known most of her life. "Short people have to make a lot of noise because we're always being overlooked."

"I refuse to believe anyone ever overlooked you." He glanced at his watch. In an entirely different tone he said, "I'm expecting a call, but before it arrives I want to talk about your situation. Will you accept the money from me to pay your hotel bill here?"

"No," she blurted, outraged.

"Why? You wouldn't have to worry about your finances. You'd have a week to explore London, and then go home on the ticket you already have."

He made it sound as though it was a perfectly normal thing to do. Indeed, from his point of view, a week's hotel bill would be insignificant.

Yet Siena couldn't do it.

"No," she said more temperately. "I'm not accepting money from you, and I have to get home as soon as I can."

He inspected her with chilling dispassion. "So you can hold Gemma's hand and tell her everything's fine, that stealing your fiancé is nothing to worry about? Don't you think it's time she grew up and stopped relying on you so much?"

Siena blinked, but said fiercely, "I *want* to go home."

Nick shrugged. "I'm heading for Hong Kong this afternoon. You can come with me if you want to."

Wondering if she'd heard right, she stared at him.

His expression was as unreadable as ever, but his tone was hard and cold. "This must be the first time I've ever seen you without an answer. A simple yes or no will suffice."

Buying time, she asked, "Why?"

"Why am I going? On business—I'm meeting there with a Chinese government delegation."

"I can't just go winging off to Hong Kong with you," she managed, her leaping heart shortening her breath.

"Why not? Chances are this will be your fastest way home."

The formidable authority of his tone told her he'd closed the door on last night's episode. Wish-

ing fervently she could keep her life in compart-
ments too, Siena opened her mouth to object.

Then closed it again when Nick continued,
"The meeting will take all tomorrow, and after
that I'm travelling on to New Zealand, so you'll
have time for a very quick look around Hong
Kong. Have you ever been there?"

She shook her head. "It sounds great," she said,
ignoring the temptation that licked seductively
through her, fogging her brain. "But not even
you will be able to get last-minute tickets to the
other side of the world, especially when there's
no emergency, and anyway, I can't afford—"

"It won't cost you anything—or me. I have an
interest in the plane," he said calmly, as though
it was the most normal thing in the world.

Siena blinked, then gave a wry smile. "Of
course you have." She took a deep breath. It would
be far too dangerous to her peace of mind to go
anywhere with him. "What about a hotel…?"

She registered a fleeting look of steel and her
words trailed away.

"If you're wondering if I intend to seduce you,

relax," he said, in a voice that sent a pang of shame though her. "You'll be perfectly safe. You want to get back home, and I'm heading in that direction, with a business stopover. It's the most sensible thing for you to do."

Siena bit her lip, with difficulty holding back the words *I'm not a charity case*. Boldly facing him, she said, "Of course I don't think you'd try anything—well, *anything*." Colour heated her skin but she went on, "It's just—I don't want to be a nuisance."

"Trust me, you'll be less of a nuisance where I can keep an eye on you than alone here in London with your money running out. I have a suite in one of the big Hong Kong hotels so it will cost me nothing extra to have you with me."

The tinge of acid in his voice deepened the colour in her cheeks.

Before she could think of anything to say he continued blandly, "Besides, your parents would be concerned to think of you alone here with rapidly dwindling resources."

Siena snorted. "You're a master manipulator,

but that one won't work. I'm not only twenty-four, I'm also more than capable of looking after myself, and they know it. So should you."

Nick stiffened. She couldn't have used a more ill-chosen word; it touched a sore point he'd never been able to overcome. His skill at manipulation was not one he was proud of, and he only ever used it as a last resort. For Siena to home in on it angered him in some obscure way.

After his idiotic behaviour last night he was crazy to even consider this, but there was no way he'd leave her on her own in London after such painful news. Normally he wasn't prey to irrational protectiveness, after all he'd do the same for her sister.

Crisply he said, "You might be sure you can take on the world single-handed, but from now on the airways will be choked with planes carrying Australians and New Zealanders back home for Christmas and the holidays."

Clearly that hadn't occurred to her. She frowned, and he went on, "You've got about as much chance of scoring an early seat as you have of swimming home."

"It's only the beginning of December," she said curtly. "It can't be that bad. Nick, you don't need to worry about me—it simply isn't necessary."

He could simply bundle her up and carry her off, but he knew Siena. She'd announce her predicament—loudly and decisively—to the first official person she saw. Not for the first time Nick cursed his stupidity the previous night. If he hadn't kissed her she'd have trusted him and accompanied him without any qualms.

That loss of trust affected him in some strange way he wasn't prepared to examine.

"I'll have to let your parents know," he said quietly.

That stopped her. He went on, "If they were at home you'd let them know what has happened."

Her slender black brows knotted. "That's not the point."

Nick pressed his advantage home. "It is, and you know it. I value your parents' good opinion.

I know what their reaction would be if I didn't tell them."

Those amazing eyes—so dark a blue they were almost violet—glittered. She stared at him as though he were an enemy.

Having learned patience the hard way, Nick knew when to wait.

She expelled a short, sharp breath. "All right, you win. I'll travel with you. Thank you for making the offer."

The final few words raced out, as though she'd had to force them through a tight throat. Her reluctance was almost palpable.

Nick took care to keep his voice level and uninflected. "Good, that's settled. Do you want me to organise the transfer of your luggage?"

"No," she said crisply. "I can do that." She hesitated a moment, then gave him a reluctant smile. "Thanks, Nick. You might feel you owe something to Dad for his mentorship all those years ago, but now you can consider it paid."

For some reason that irritated him. "I'm not repaying any supposed debt. It's simply the most sensible path to take." He paused, then asked, "What do you plan to do when you get back?"

"Find another job," she said briefly. "I don't like the insecurity of wondering how fast my bank balance is going down."

"I meant about Adrian Worth."

Her luscious mouth tightened. "Nothing."

"No recriminations?" Nick wasn't entirely sure why he was pushing her but he wanted an answer.

"It would be a waste of time," she said, sounding detached. "It's over."

Nick gave a mental shrug. The man was clearly an idiot, and she was doing the right thing in cutting her losses.

"Right," he said briskly. "The car will take you back to the hotel and wait for you there."

Siena stared around at what looked like nothing so much as a very modern, very opulent sitting room.

"I thought…" she began, then stopped.

When Nick told her he had an interest in the plane she'd foolishly thought he meant he had shares in the airline. It hadn't occurred to her they'd be travelling halfway around the world in a sleek, luxurious private jet.

The only two passengers...

The implied intimacy worried her. But lying in wait beneath the concern was a lurking excitement, and that worried her even more.

She felt like an ancient explorer in an unknown country, not knowing what lay ahead, aware only that she might be walking into danger...

For a moment her heart misgave her, but sturdily she pushed the apprehension to the back of her mind. Those ancient explorers had also found untold riches.

After customs and immigration formalities they'd been driven out to the plane parked outside an opulent reception area, and while their luggage was loaded and efficiently packed away the steward had shown them into the main cabin, exquisitely furnished with the kind of effortless luxury known only to plutocrats. It was set up to be what estate agents called "a media room", with sofas and a large television screen.

Siena was determined to appreciate the whole experience. It would be the only time in her life she travelled like this.

Nick indicated a couple of chairs side by side, their sole concession to airline safety the seatbelts neatly arranged across them. "We're almost ready to go, so sit down and fasten the seatbelt. And what exactly *did* you think?"

"I didn't realise we were travelling privately." But she sat down, her stomach fluttering.

Nick examined her face with a frown. "Would you rather be in a big plane?"

"No. I'm not afraid of flying." The treacherous pulse throbbing in her throat was due entirely to his closeness. Hastily she said, "I'm just not used to such luxury. But don't worry, I plan to enjoy it to the full."

He sat down beside her and asked, "Did you get all your emails off?"

Siena pulled herself together. "Yes—and an answer from Dad."

"You're a close-knit family."

It was the sort of thing any friend might say,

but a note in his voice caught her attention. Perhaps it was also the sort of thing the product of a broken home might say. Did Nick have any relatives at all? He'd never mentioned any. She did know his mother had died shortly after Nick had bought her a home overlooking the harbour on Auckland's North Shore. Almost immediately afterwards Nick had left New Zealand.

Without looking at him, Siena said, "I needed to tell them about the change of plans."

She'd also laboured over a very short, extremely difficult email to her ex-fiancé, about whom she'd somehow developed an uneasy guilt.

If only she hadn't kissed Nick, she thought, then caught herself up. She couldn't blame him for her suspicion that she'd somehow short-changed Adrian.

While she'd been struggling with the email, the prospect of spending a night in Hong Kong with Nick had kept intruding, bringing with it such a turbulent combination of excitement and foreboding that she'd felt like a hypocrite.

In the end she had forced herself to finish what had turned out to be a banal, stiff note.

Nick asked, "How are your parents enjoying their cruise?"

"They're having a glorious time. Dad's checked out every deck game and the library, and Mum's made several friends already. And they've danced until the small hours each night."

"And how is Gemma?"

Siena felt the jet begin to move. She looked out of the window, saying a silent goodbye to London.

"She sounds much better." She glanced at him and then away. "She's very sensitive."

His raised brows irritated her, but the jet's engines picked up speed and the plane began to move down the runway. Relieved, Siena leaned forward a little, watching the earth fall away as they finally soared into the hazy air.

A strange sensation gripped her, as though she'd left her everyday life behind and somehow slipped through into another dimension, one both exhilarating and rather ominous, a place where the dictates of ordinary life were suspended. Unbidden and unwanted, a feverish anticipation licked through her, summoning dangerous thoughts.

Perhaps this was what travelling in a private jet did, she thought fancifully.

Be sensible, she warned herself, and asked, "Do you always travel in your own plane?"

"Usually. It saves time and hassle, gives me space to work while I'm travelling, and generally is simpler all round."

"I'll say!" Siena sighed. "This trip is going to spoil me for ordinary travel."

Nick's smile held more than a hint of irony. "I doubt it." He glanced at his watch. "I find it helps to avoid jet-lag if when I board I start operating on the current time at my destination. Once we reach cruising height I've ordered tea, but would you prefer something else to drink?"

"Tea will be lovely, thank you," she said gratefully, pulling out a book from her bag. "If you want to work, go ahead. I don't need entertaining."

"I remember," he said, amused again.

Siena gave him a sideways look, not exactly relishing the way he'd slotted her neatly back into her place of childhood friend.

He was still watching her, and although the smile that curved his chiselled mouth didn't waver, she sensed a keener intensity in his green survey.

What was he thinking?

Who knew? Nick had always had a poker face; it had been one of the things she'd first noticed about him, an unchildlike refusal to show emotion. Now she found herself speculating about the source of that fierce self-control.

It seemed possible that Nick's cool, complete self-containment had originally hidden the sort of trauma no child should ever endure.

But perhaps his self-control was inborn, an essential part of the boy he'd been and the man he now was.

Nick said, "I do need to work, but I'll wait until the seatbelt sign goes off."

Hastily Siena buried herself in her book, religiously reading until a ping announced they'd reached cruising altitude and Nick got up.

"I'll work at the desk," he said. "If you need anything, the steward will deal with it."

She'd noticed the desk at the other end of the cabin. From beneath her lashes she watched Nick walk across to it and open up a drawer to take out a laptop.

He was a surprising—and unusual—amalgam of magnate and sex symbol. Filmstar good-looks were intensified and overwhelmed by an earthy, potent aura that gave them a raw edge. In casual clothes obviously tailored to his measurements he dominated the trappings of extreme wealth without effort, reducing them to a mere backdrop.

He was, she thought, nerves tightening in sensual appreciation, a dangerous man.

And her attitude to him was veering uncomfortably and recklessly close to absorption.

CHAPTER FIVE

HALF an hour into the flight Siena gave up on the thriller she'd been enjoying. For the past thirty minutes her eyes had skimmed words that made little impression, and she'd completely lost sympathy with the hero and heroine.

She closed the book, got up and walked across to the sofa facing the television screen, lowering herself onto the seat.

"If you want to turn on the TV," Nick said, "go ahead."

She flashed him a smile, her stomach knotting as their eyes met. "No, thanks, but if you want to…"

"I haven't finished here," he said, and returned his attention to the computer screen.

Siena picked up a magazine and flicked over the pages. It was exactly what she'd have expected on a private jet, catering to an exclusive readership with money to burn.

But both the photography and the writing were superb. Her attention caught, she read an article about a castle in the Pyrenees before moving onto a rhapsodic description of a spa in Bali. Admiring the rooms and courtyards that combined restraint and tropical exuberance, she decided that one day she'd visit that exquisite island with its tropical flowers and gentle people. Perhaps.

When she'd found a job and saved the money.

A little later, deep in pictures of impossibly manicured rice paddies climbing mountains, she heard someone cough.

Looking up, she saw the steward coming with a trolley.

"Tea, Ms Blake," he said. "May I…?"

He showed her the trolley. Just like high tea at a very good hotel, she thought, smiling at the memory of the one time she'd been treated to such an occasion.

She looked across to Nick, who glanced up

from his computer and said, "English Breakfast, no milk or sugar, and whatever else looks good."

Choose for him? She remembered him devouring her mother's chocolate cake and pavlova, New Zealand's classic meringue confection decorated with kiwifruit slices, but apart from that she had no idea of his tastes.

So she smiled at the steward and said, "Just leave the trolley, thanks."

When Nick sat down beside her she poured tea and handed his cup to him, making sure she didn't touch his fingers.

To fill in the silence she said chattily, "This reminds me that after my capping ceremony Mum and Dad took us all—several friends—to a hotel and shouted us high tea. We drank champagne first, and ate little delicacies like these sandwiches and scones." She laughed as she added milk to her own cup. "And the waiter was so busy staring at Gemma he almost tipped champagne down my front, all over the robes I'd hired for the day."

The corners of Nick's mouth twitched. "Very

unprofessional of him," he said somewhat austerely.

"Ah, well, if you go out with Gemma you get used to that sort of thing. It was a great day." She smiled, recalling her excitement and joy.

He said, "I tried damned hard to get there, but I had an emergency on my hands and I couldn't make it."

She'd been disappointed, but also just a little relieved. "Trust the world's finances to collapse the month I graduated."

"You didn't want to do postgraduate study?"

She shook her head. "You weren't the only one dealing with a financial meltdown. Dad and Mum had helped me enough. Anyway, I wanted to get out into the real world and do some work."

"So you started in a plant nursery—after taking a commerce degree."

The faint note of surprise in his voice produced a shrug that probably seemed a bit defensive. "I like gardens and plants. In fact, I tossed up about taking a landscaping course before I settled on commerce. And I really liked the woman who hired me. Furthermore, she needed me."

"Why?"

"Her husband had just died, and he'd always looked after the business side of things. She was a gardener, not a businesswoman, and she was lost and afraid and grieving. So she was more than happy to let me take over the management of the place while she dealt with the plants."

"I'm not in the least surprised," he said dryly, and selected a sandwich from the tiered stand. "You have an air of competence that must have been very reassuring to a woman dealing with widowhood."

"Well, thank you," she said, surprised. "Nick, I seem to remember you used to love scones. I don't, so why don't you eat them all?"

He laughed, and for a moment she saw the boy who'd teased two small girls, taught them games and asked them riddles, comforted Gemma when she'd been bullied about her height at school, climbed to Siena's aid when she'd got herself stuck halfway up a big jacaranda tree, and warned her about overestimating her ability to swim long distances...

With adults he'd been wary and controlled until over the years her father's cheerful pleasure in his company had slowly won acceptance.

Which might have meant that before he'd become a part of their lives he'd discovered it wasn't safe to trust adults.

"That," he said on a coolly questioning note, "is a very intent look. Did you want the scones after all?"

"No!" she expostulated, and laughed, feeling strangely as though she'd been caught out. "Just don't think you can get away with eating all the club sandwiches."

He seemed to relax. "You always did have a hearty appetite. I used to wonder where you put it, but it wasn't long before I realised you ran it off. It's good to see a woman who isn't picky about her food."

"Now you've made me feel greedy." She sighed and added, "But I'm still going to have that cup-cake, even though it will be like eating a work of art. Do you remember Mum used to slice the tops off and cut them in two, then use whipped cream to glue the halves on like wings?"

"I do indeed," he said. "You called them butterfly cakes."

She laughed. "And I remember that once you ate five of them. I was hugely impressed."

Later, she sat on the side of a big double bed in the larger of the two bedrooms. Except that they were probably called cabins, she thought with a hint of a smile. Far from being ostentatious or blatant, the interior had been fitted out with an eye to welcoming comfort. Her room even boasted an *en suite* bathroom, as elegant and efficient as that in Nick's house.

In her chain-store pyjamas she was definitely out of place—as alien as she would be on a space ship. And she was way out of her league.

Had the Nick she remembered ever really existed? Occasionally she saw flashes of that boy, but underlying the fragile link of shared childhood experiences smouldered something else, something hard-edged and very, very basic.

Sudden tears burnt the back of her eyes. She had the weird feeling she'd never known herself, that the woman who'd become engaged to Adrian—made love with him, planned a future with him—had been acting a part.

With Nick she felt stimulated, aroused, elated—more alive, more…

Just *more*. Blinking hard, she looked around, eyes roaming the soothing blues and creams of the room.

And she'd better get over that feeling, because she didn't belong here. This was Nick's world now, but it had never been hers. And it never would be.

When he married—if he ever did—he'd choose someone who fitted into this existence of jetting from one side of the world to another in the utmost luxury. Any interest he might have in her clearly wasn't going to be acted on; after that kiss he'd made no attempt to touch her. Her position as her father's daughter meant he didn't consider her as…what?

A candidate for the position of lover?

"Oh, come off it," she muttered beneath her breath. Nick could have almost any woman in the world…why would he choose her?

A knock on her door startled her. She opened her mouth to call *Come in*, but closed it when she caught sight of herself in the full-length mirror. Her skimpy singlet top and shorts revealed almost as much white skin as her nakedness last night.

Hastily she got up and huddled into the dressing gown—several sizes too large—hung for her to use. Her heart pounding a sudden tattoo, she opened the door.

Nick stood there. He examined her with suddenly intent eyes. "You've been crying."

"I—no, not really," she said foolishly, resisting the urge to take a step back. Swathed in white towelling she had to look like a kid in dressing-up clothes, and he seemed to loom over her.

When he reached out she froze, her breath locking in her chest as her eyes widened.

He brushed the skin beneath one eye, a touch so light she should barely have felt it. Instead it registered in every cell in her body, fierce as a lightning strike, potent as an age-old curse.

Seductive as sunlight and champagne on a summer's evening…

Tension tightened her throat but she managed to say hoarsely, "It's all right. I'm not going to howl all over you again. Did you want something?"

"Just to make sure you have everything you need." His voice was curt, each word bitten off as though he was angry.

"Yes, thank you." It sounded stiff and abrupt, but she didn't dare say anything else.

Clearly it was enough. "Good. I'll see you in the morning."

And he turned away.

Siena closed the door with a small click and leaned back against it, sombrely eyeing herself in the mirror. She looked like a…

"A dormouse," she muttered between her teeth. "A white dormouse out of a children's book."

She shrugged off the gown and hung it up again, then crawled into the bed, turned off the lights and lay contemplating the ceiling, the steady sound of the jet's engines a background to her thoughts.

One thing she'd always prided herself on was her common sense, and now was the time to call on it. Only an idiot would moon over a man who was doing his utmost to show her how much he regretted kissing her. Nick might even be rueing his offer to convey her back to New Zealand. Certainly he'd only made the suggestion because she was her father's daughter.

Her mouth firmed. No more foolishness.

From this very moment she'd enjoy the unaccustomed luxury, relish the visit to Hong Kong—and keep reminding herself she was merely a childhood acquaintance of Nick's, nothing more.

She'd scarcely thought of Adrian since she'd got on the plane. Was she going to cut him out of her heart so swiftly—so easily? It made a mockery of everything she'd believed, everything she'd felt. She hated to believe she was so shallow and faithless, but unpalatable or not, it seemed she was.

* * *

The words on the screen seemed to jump, and after a glance at the time Nick pressed "Save" and "Quit" and got to his feet. His first meeting with the Chinese delegation was less than two hours after the plane arrived in Hong Kong, so he needed to be on top form.

And that meant sleep. But excess energy seethed through him, demanding release. What he really needed was a workout, an hour spent forcing his body past its limits and into exhaustion.

Mouth set in a grim line, he strode to the other bedroom. A shower eased muscles set too long in one position, and once in bed he stretched the few remaining kinks out of his long limbs. Normally he'd have slept immediately, but as the jet droned on towards Hong Kong he found himself lying awake, an image of Siena in the far-too-large dressing gown curling his mouth in a smile.

Not for long, however. His expression hardened as he faced an extremely unpalatable truth. Even swathed in what had seemed acres of white fabric, he'd wanted her.

He still wanted her. Hunger ached through his body like a sweet fever, one that had lain quiescent for years only to ambush him the moment he'd seen Siena again.

Not for the first time he cursed his weakness.

He could—perhaps—have understood if it was her sister who affected him like that, yet Gemma's beauty left him completely cold.

Five years ago, when he'd lost his head and made love to Siena, it had felt like coming home. Afterwards, while she slept in his arms, he'd fought a desperate fight against the prospect that this overwhelming feeling for her might be love. Angry at his loss of control, he'd forced himself to ignore her warmth and soft litheness, the sense of completeness he'd never felt before.

Love was a danger he'd not foreseen. He knew about love, had lived all his life with its other, hidden face; he'd seen too much of the havoc it could create. It held people prisoner, kept them a willing slave to another's cruelty.

And five years ago not only had he been immature but he'd had an empire to rule, a future to create—a future where his emotions were kept under strict control.

A future that—until a few days ago, when Siena burst into it like a small tornado—had been lived on his terms. Although he'd always given and demanded fidelity in his relationships, he'd never expected or wanted emotional commitment. His life had satisfied him completely until now, when it suddenly seemed barren.

But he still regretted his abrupt abandonment of her after their night together. Restlessly he turned his head on a pillow that seemed too hot, too soft.

So why had he let himself lower his guard and take that kiss? She'd just been dumped by her fiancé, so the last thing she'd needed was for someone she trusted to make a move on her.

Even if she were willing…

Even if she *were* willing, he wasn't interested in standing in for someone else, being used to banish another man's image from her mind and heart.

If she came to him, he wanted everything.

Where the *hell* had that thought come from?

From the same place, he decided grimly, that had suggested he offer her this trip to Hong Kong. He should have paid for her to fly first class back to New Zealand instead of bringing her—a delicious, desirable and damned dangerous irritant—with him.

Except that she wouldn't have accepted such an offer, and he had no way to force or persuade her to.

Anyway, it was only for two days. After they got back to New Zealand they could resume the distance they'd kept for the past five years.

At least he'd have her co-operation. Apart from her wild response to his kiss she'd been pleasantly distant, without a hint of fluttering lashes, no lingering glances or significant silences.

He frowned, punched his pillow with more force than was necessary, and settled down to summon sleep, slowly sliding into a dream where Siena faded into a dark distance that swallowed her up.

* * *

Feeling rather like an extra on a film set, Siena waited until she was alone with Nick before allowing herself to gaze around the sitting room in the hotel suite. Arriving in Hong Kong with him had been almost surreal.

Met at the airport by a limousine, they'd been driven through teeming streets to a hotel parking area with its own lift. There they'd been greeted by a smartly suited man who'd accompanied them to the penthouse suite and checked them in.

All very private and discreet...

Now the door had closed, she turned slowly to take in the huge room, furnished with a superb collection of classic colonial furniture mingled with magnificent Chinese pieces. The skilful blend of colours and forms made for a tranquil haven far above those busy streets.

Withdrawing her gaze from what was probably a priceless antique Chinese cabinet, she glanced across the room at Nick. Her heart jumped and she felt his formidable impact right down to her toes.

Tall, immaculately dressed in casual clothes,

his hawkish features not softened by a smile that held more than a hint of sardonic appreciation, he was completely at home in all this sophisticated beauty.

Hastily she said, "I didn't think anything could outdo the plane, but this—" she flung out her arms to encompass the room "—this is *amazing*. Stunningly lovely without being ostentatious."

"It's all part of the image—very important in some areas of the world. Check out the view. Hong Kong does views magnificently."

His calm voice made her feel she was overreacting.

From a wide balcony she absorbed a breathtaking panorama over Hong Kong—the harbour streaked by the wakes of a multitude of boats, and all around towering buildings that almost blocked out a backdrop of forested hills.

"Beautiful and very impressive," she said. "And so—so *vibrant*! I'm buzzing as though someone's given me a double shot of adrenalin!" She turned to find him barely a pace behind her. Again her heart somersaulted. *Be sensible,* she ordered it.

He asked, "How are you feeling? Tired?"

"Wonderful! Nothing—believe me, *nothing*—like I did after I reeled out of cattle class in Heathrow several days ago." She shuddered, and took the opportunity to step sideways, keeping her gaze fixed on a ferry bumbling across the harbour.

"I should hope not," Nick said, taking his time about inspecting her face. "The whole idea of private jets is to get their human cargo to a destination in as good a condition as possible."

Colour washed delicately up through her skin. "They do the job well."

"You look better," he observed. "To use a cliché, as fresh as a daisy."

All Siena could think of was a boring, "So do you." And because his nearness was kindling tiny brushfires in every nerve she added with a brief smile, "I need to unpack."

"A maid will do that for you." He glanced at his watch. "I've ordered a meal, and after that I'll be in a meeting for the rest of the day. What would you like to do to fill the time?"

"Look around," she said promptly. "I saw some sort of market not very far from the hotel."

"I'll get someone to organise a trip there for you."

Taken aback, she said, "I won't need that—I can walk."

Nick's brows met above his arrogant nose. "You've never been here before, and trust me—it'll be more fun bargaining with a local on your side."

Matching his frown with one of her own, she began, "Nick—"

"Siena, humour me, will you?"

Made uneasy by a treacherous desire to do just that, she drew a breath and ploughed on. "I've always believed this was a safe city."

He didn't hesitate. "Hong Kong is fairly safe, but if you take someone with you who knows the market you'll certainly see more, and it will cost you less than if you try to buy on your own. New Zealanders are notoriously bad at bargaining."

"But it will cost *you* to hire someone—"

With words that held a harsh undertone, he cut

in, "Your father never thought of cost or prices when he took me around as a kid. In fact, you children probably missed out on treats because of me—I know things were pretty tight financially for most of your childhood. It's thanks to him I can afford to do what I like now, and what I like right now is making sure you're looked after."

Which well and truly put her firmly in her place, Siena thought, strangely hurt. He *was* doing this out of some misplaced idea of repaying her father.

Although she'd been almost certain of that from the moment he'd offered her this trip home, having it confirmed so bluntly chilled her.

She didn't dare let herself stumble into emotional danger. Every woman Nick had ever been linked with had been gorgeous, so clearly he took beauty for granted when it came to his affairs. Although Siena knew she was reasonably attractive in her own way, she winced at the damning words, for when had *reasonably attractive* ever challenged *gorgeous* and won?

But, lovely though his women had been, he'd never married.

She'd made a mistake with Adrian. She had no intention—ever—of making an even bigger, more reckless mistake about Nick, no matter how sexy and exciting he might be.

"Siena," Nick said, something in his tone telling her he was losing patience, "I can't, of course, force you take someone with you, but I'd be much happier if you did."

Chin lifting, she met his eyes and saw that behind the uncompromising command lay entreaty—clearly he felt he had to do this for her. Although it irked her to surrender, and her smile probably showed too many teeth to be entirely convincing, she conceded, "Oh, all right then. Bring on your bargaining expert and tour guide."

"How much money do you have?"

Siena cast her eyes heavenward. "If things here are as cheap as I've heard, I'm OK. I charged my card before I left, and thanks to you I'll have a refund waiting for me when I get back from my plane ticket."

"How much in Hong Kong currency?"

She stared at him, then sighed. "None," she admitted reluctantly. "Can I get some at Reception?"

Nick's smile was narrow and sharp. "You'd rather do that than take money from me?" When Siena hesitated he said, "It's called cutting off your nose to spite your face."

"Oh, all *right*," she said crossly. "I'll pay you back at today's rate."

He extracted a wallet, peeled off a wad of notes and held them out.

"Thank you, but I wish it wasn't necessary."

His face hardened, but he shrugged and in a crisp tone said, "Stop seeing yourself as being a nuisance. And have fun."

CHAPTER SIX

FOUR hours later—hot and tired and thoroughly pleased with herself—Siena spread out a swag of ridiculously cheap purchases on the sofa in her bedroom and examined them again. She and the older woman who'd appeared to escort her had shopped carefully, and thanks to the other woman's hard-nosed bargaining her hoard of gifts had cost her an astonishingly small amount.

A knock on the door lifted her head. Sternly telling her racing pulse to calm down, she called, "Come in."

Nick pushed open the door. One sweep of green eyes took in her purchases before fixing on her.

"Enjoy yourself?" he asked, his tone neutral.

She produced a smile. "You were right. Grace Lam was a huge help. So you have my permission to gloat all you like. And I probably would have got lost."

"Handsome of you to admit it," he said, humour glinting in his eyes.

"But I'd have found my way back again," she retorted immediately.

This time he flung back his head and laughed. "Of course you would have—eventually. Mind if I take a look?"

"No," she said, and told him who each object was for, finishing, "And this dog barks when you press its stomach. It's for the little girl next door at home. She's got mumps, poor poppet, so she might like a soft toy."

Siena paused, then said, "Grace—my guide— told me you'd suggested we go out tomorrow again, and she thought I might enjoy the Heritage Museum."

"A good idea."

Siena nodded. "Either that or the Wetlands Park, which I'd like to see too, because quite a lot of New Zealand's migratory birds stop off there on their way to and from the Arctic. Have you been to either place?"

"Both. If I were you I'd go to the museum. It's fascinating and very Hong Kong."

"OK," she said.

His mouth quirked.

"What's so surprising?" she challenged.

Broad shoulders moved in the slightest of shrugs. In a voice that came close to deadpan, he said, "I suppose I've become accustomed to hearing you object rather than agree."

She gave him a startled look, then felt ashamed. "Have I been behaving like a spoilt kid?"

"More like someone determined to assert her independence."

"Now I feel like a snotty little adolescent," she said thoughtfully. "I'm sorry. I'm really grateful—"

"I don't want your gratitude," he cut in, his tone flinty.

Taken aback, she said, "Then I won't mention it again. But I'll bow to your superior knowledge of Hong Kong, so the museum it will be."

"I've finished for the day, so I thought we'd have dinner and then go up the Peak." At her baffled look he said, "Every visitor to Hong Kong goes up Victoria Peak—it's obligatory, and the view is astonishing, both day and night."

"That would be great." Sightseeing was a nice safe thing to do. No doubt there'd be lots of people around, and it would take up the evening and give her something more sensible to think of than the fierce, disturbing excitement that gripped her whenever she saw Nick.

"Would you rather eat here or in a restaurant?"

"A restaurant," she said rapidly, because that wouldn't be as intimate as dinner in the suite. But she felt compelled to say, "Unless you're tired and would rather eat here?"

He didn't look tired, but he'd been working all day.

Obviously amused, he shook his head. "You sound just like your mother. I'm not tired. Where would you like to go? There are several superb restaurants in the hotel, and thousands of very good ones in Hong Kong. How do you feel about local food?"

"Yes, please," she said promptly. *She sounded like her mother?*

If she'd needed anything more to prove he wasn't in the least interested in her, that throwaway comment had done it.

Stiffly she said, "Let me treat you to it. That's if they'll take my card."

Nick looked at her, and to her astonishment smiled and said, "They'll take any card. All right, then, and thank you. One of the small places down the street is excellent. Or would you prefer—?"

"A small one would be great," she broke in, thinking of her one good dress.

While she'd been learning bargaining skills at the market someone had unpacked her clothes, pressed them and stored them carefully in the massive wardrobe. Even so, the blue dress looked tired.

However, she put it on. This would possibly be the only time she ever went out with Nick.

Hastily she squelched that thought before it turned into useless regret. And when they walked into the restaurant she realised she could have worn jeans and no one would have noticed. The place seemed to be favoured by locals—some in what seemed to be working gear, some in sophisticated designer gear. The few tourists were more casually dressed.

"How did you know about this restaurant?" she asked curiously.

"It was recommended to me the first time I came to Hong Kong," Nick told her as they were ushered to a table.

"Do you eat here often?"

"Whenever I'm in the city."

Which made her realise that all she knew of his life away from New Zealand was what she'd read in various gossip magazines and the financial pages.

You're very peripheral in his life, she thought. *Just remember that...*

Nick ordered a dinner of several savoury, spicy dishes, some fried, some steamed, all delicious.

Later she'd be impressed by his wide knowledge and considered opinions and views; at the time she made sure she tried all the dishes and concentrated on the atmosphere. Too much attention to Nick could only be dangerous.

Not that her studied restraint was easy. Each time his glance collided with hers—blue clashing with green—a sensuous, tantalising reaction licked inconveniently through her.

"Enjoying yourself?" he asked once.

"Very much," she returned, keeping her voice light. "This food is a revelation."

Yet again her foolish pulse galloped into overdrive when he returned her smile with a somewhat saturnine one of his own.

But all he said was, "Hong Kong loves food and is famous for it. If you've finished we'll head for the Peak. For your first visit it's obligatory to go by tram."

After one look at the rails Siena braced herself for a steep upward journey, vowing for possibly the tenth time that evening not to allow herself to be so incandescently aware of Nick—as though every sense receptor in her body and brain was focused on him only.

Once they'd disembarked she looked around at the crowd who'd decided to highlight their evening with a trip to the Peak. Many were tourists, and most of the women strolling by took in Nick's dominating presence at her side.

She tried very hard to be amused when they transferred their attention to her, their appreciation frequently turning to slight puzzlement.

You're here for the view, she reminded herself. *Concentrate on it.*

It was worth it—an astonishing, multicoloured, layered explosion of lights and tall buildings and ferries plying across the harbour, with all that splendour of light and colour eventually fading into the textured darkness of the hills behind.

"Oh, my goodness," she breathed. "Oh, this is amazing. How high are we?"

"Over twelve hundred feet—four hundred metres," Nick told her.

She took in a deep breath of warm air. "You know, mingled with that fresh green-leaf perfume from the bush I think I can smell the scent of millions of delicious meals. How many people live here?"

"Give or take a thousand or two, about eight million—double New Zealand's population on approximately a thousand square kilometres." He paused before adding, "And, in spite of all those people crammed into such a small area, most of Hong Kong is still forested."

Nick looked down at her. Her exquisite skin was slightly flushed, and she pushed a clinging black curl away from her neck. After England's winter gloom she was probably feeling the heat, although the arrival of evening had banished the cloying humidity of a Hong Kong summer.

She was gazing at the glittering panorama beneath them, absorbed in its ever-changing beauty. Would she look the same if he showed her Petra, rose-red and ancient in the desert, or the sensuous stone glories of Angkor Wat beneath the clogging tenacity of the oriental jungle?

Turning to him, she said, "You've obviously done your research."

"I always research," he told her.

The more you knew, the fewer surprises you had to deal with—a lesson he'd learned very early in life.

"Somehow I'm not surprised." She gave him a teasing half-smile. "Knowledge is power, right?"

Nick felt something tug at his gut—a swift hunger, the potent forerunner of lust.

Abruptly he asked, "Seen enough?"

She glanced away, eyes smoky and huge in her face. "Yes, for the moment. But one day I'll come back here."

With whom?

Surprised by that thought, Nick heard her finish, "And I bet you have a busy day ahead tomorrow."

For some strange reason he was touched. He couldn't remember any of his lovers showing concern for his wellbeing.

Not that they'd had reason to worry about his stamina, he thought wryly.

And wondered why memories of previous love-making seemed slightly tawdry, as though in an odd way he'd been unfaithful. To Siena...? Impossible.

On the way back to the hotel he took care to keep things superficial. As they walked through the impressive doors the distant strain of music filtered through the lobby. Siena turned her head towards it.

"The nightclub," he told her laconically. And startled himself by saying, "They hold Thirties nights—foxtrots and waltzes and so on. Would you like to go in?"

He'd surprised her, too. After a quick upward glance and a moment of hesitation she said doubtfully, "We're not exactly dressed for it."

"I don't think anyone will notice. Or care."

She sent him one of her sparkling glances. "I suspect you're insinuating that you're so well known—or so rich—you can go anywhere you like and be welcome." She shook her black curls sadly at him. "Such arrogance. My mother—and yours, from what I remember of her—would be shocked to the core."

His mouth quirked. "Shall we see?"

"Why not? I'd like to be able to say I danced here once."

As he'd known would happen, the doorman took one look at Nick and said, "Delighted to see you, Mr Grenville."

Siena waited until they were seated on a secluded banquette to say, "Don't tell me they recognise everyone staying here."

Only the very rich, Nick thought. Somehow she made him feel jaded. He shrugged it off and said coolly, "I've been here before."

"I'm assuming you didn't do the rock star thing—trash the room so they'd remember you?"

"Not my style."

She gave him a glimmering smile. "Oh, you're so right. You've always been completely in control."

Nick ordered drinks—champagne for her and a beer for himself. At her incredulous glance he said easily, "You can take the bloke out of New Zealand…"

"…but you can't New Zealand out of the bloke,"

she finished, her sunny gurgle of laughter catching him in some previously invulnerable place.

His sinews tightened and he fought back a memory of the kiss he'd given her. No, the kiss they'd exchanged; she'd been right there with him.

But not for long.

Her laughter had attracted the attention of a couple of young men at the next table. Nick noted their appreciative glances, and for a second he resented their presence so strongly he had to cover his reaction by saying tersely, "I made my first big deal here, and afterwards drank beer in my hotel room to celebrate. Since then I've always had a glass."

"For sentimental reasons?"

"For sentimental reasons," he agreed.

Siena was astounded, but her response was interrupted by surely the fastest waiter in the world arriving with their drinks.

"So here's to Hong Kong. And to home," Nick said evenly, and drank.

Siena sipped the champagne and set her glass

down. "Just as well I'm not spending too much time here with you," she told him lazily. "I could get used to this ambience."

A couple walked in, the woman tall, slender, exquisitely gowned in something that breathed Paris couture. Pearls hung around her throat, and on one slender finger she sported a gem the size of a canary's egg.

"Goodness," Siena said in a stunned voice. "She's just a tad overdressed, don't you think? Surely that's not a diamond? And are those pearls *real*?"

Nick didn't have a chance to answer, because the couple saw them and turned towards their table. He stood, his expression unmoving.

Hoping fervently they hadn't overheard her comment, Siena fell silent.

"Dear Nick," the woman said affectionately when they stopped by the table. Her smile didn't warm the porcelain perfection of her face as her eyes swept over Siena, probably pricing her dress to within a cent. "How lovely to see you here."

The middle-aged man with the newcomer said,

"Nick, dear boy," in a deep voice, and held out his hand.

After the greetings Nick introduced Siena to the couple, whose names she didn't recognise. They responded with studied grace, but their attention was bent on Nick.

When they'd left to join a couple on the other side of the dance floor Nick said, "Sorry about that."

"This is your world," she said, realising how very much out of place she was in it. Awkwardly she went on, "If I'd known you knew them I'd have been more tactful."

Nick sketched a smile that held contempt and a touch of cruelty. "You don't need to be. My friends are a mixed bunch, but they don't include the Baron and his wife. I don't like vultures."

Shocked, Siena blinked. "Oh," she said lamely.

He said, "He made the money for those jewels from arms dealing. Whenever I look at them I see the wreckage of millions of lives."

A shiver of distaste chilled through her.

Getting lithely to his feet, he said, "Forget about

them. Let's dance. Can you do ancient dances like the waltz?"

"Of course I can," she said indignantly. "Mum made sure Gemma and I had dance lessons. But this isn't a waltz anyway."

His smile softened. "Just checking," he said laconically, and took her in his arms.

From being touched by ice Siena was transformed into a being of heat and fire. His nearness set her alight, filling her with a precarious, intense delight that mingled anticipation with a thrill of adrenalin. His arm around her back held her close, but not too close, and one hand enclosed hers. If she lifted her gaze it would linger on his arrogantly jutting jaw and the beautiful, sensual curves of his mouth.

So she kept her eyes fixed on his chest.

Trying to ignore a reckless physical longing, she concentrated on her steps—not that she needed to. Nick danced superbly, his confidence carrying her with it. Was there nothing he couldn't do? Siena racked her brains, but couldn't recall him failing in anything he'd ever tackled.

He looked down at her. "I keep forgetting how small you are. You punch above your weight."

"I have to," she said forthrightly. "Otherwise people tend to treat me like a kid. I'm really looking forward to a few wrinkles because they'll give me some gravitas."

"You might well be the only woman in the world who is," he said on a note of irony. "Tell me something: why did you settle for money instead of going through legal channels with your ex-boss?"

Her baffled glance clashed with a survey as cold and dangerous as polar ice. "Mainly because I didn't want to put Mum and Dad through any sort of court hearing. They've saved and worked all their lives to be able to afford this trip, but they'd have stayed behind to support me." She sent him a direct glance. "Which is also why I agreed to being railroaded into travelling home with you."

"I know," he said laconically.

"And a cop I know said that if I didn't have any

proof it would be difficult to get a favourable decision. I had no proof."

"So how did you manage to extract money from him?"

"He knew that if I did make a fuss it would get around, and the mud would stick. He's married." She grimaced. "So he offered me money. I thought he'd give me a cheque, but he didn't—he gave it to me in cash. I still feel dirty about it, but at least it went to a cause he'd never support."

"So, apart from losing a sum of money, he gets off scot-free. How do you know he won't try it with the next nubile woman he employs?"

Crisply—trying to convince herself—she said, "I told him I was going to warn every new employee."

He laughed quietly. "Simple, but effective. Do you think he's learned his lesson?"

"I don't know," she said reluctantly. "I hope so."

"You always had a passion for justice, but in this case I think you probably did the best thing. You can't save the world, and it's a waste of energy to try. Pick your fights carefully—that's all you can do."

"Is that what you do?" Intrigued, she looked up.

Their eyes met and something melted at the base of her spine. A sweetly urgent sensation sizzled through her, spinning her brain into a chaos of thoughts so confusing she missed a beat.

Instantly his arms tightened, pulling her into the lean, contained power of his body. He looked above her head and moved with speed and grace to steer her out of the way of a couple who were so lost in each other they might well have been alone on the floor.

He glanced down, lashes lowering, but not soon enough to hide the glitter of desire in his gaze.

Hunger pierced her with exquisite accuracy in a pulse of headstrong lightning.

It was imperative she break eye contact, but she couldn't. *Say something,* the last thinking part of her brain commanded.

Anything...

She opened her mouth, but had to swallow to

ease her parched throat before she could croak, "Yes."

Although Nick's eyes narrowed, he was fully in command of his voice. "Yes, *what*? Tell me what you want."

She wished there had been other lovers besides Adrian to give her some experience, some understanding of the rash, insistent tide that clamoured though her with a force far more potent than everyday common sense. It urged her to forget everything but the compelling hunger that fired her blood.

Unable to do the sensible thing and lie, Siena muttered, "I want this."

But Nick wasn't going to let her off so easily. "What is *this*?"

She dragged in a breath of air. "Craziness." Her mouth straightened. "But right now it's the kind of craziness I want." She paused before adding, "If you want it too."

Nick didn't say anything. He didn't need to—she felt his answer in the leap of his blood against her, the subtle tightening of his big, lithe body. Reckless joy sang a siren song through her, sweeping away any barriers, any second thoughts.

After a moment he said softly, "Oh, I want."

A desperate delight bubbled up inside her, and a fiercely primal anticipation she'd never felt before.

As they reached their table he said beneath his breath, "Let's get out of here."

Siena walked sedately beside him, struggling so hard to contain her emotions she didn't dare say anything on the way to their suite.

As though recognising this, Nick too didn't speak.

But once inside the suite common sense made a doomed attempt to rescue her. *What on earth do you think you're doing?*

Going mad, she decided recklessly. *And I don't care.* Perhaps this might get him out of her system once and for all, with no expectations, no hope of permanence, nothing in mind but pleasure.

And if it didn't?

I'll deal with it...

"Having second thoughts?" Nick asked.

How could he be so...so cool? He didn't sound as though he'd be angry—or even irritated—if she called a halt.

Indecision drove her gaze to his face. It was set in angular lines, his mouth hard, but when she met his eyes—narrowed and predatory—a huge surge of relief washed through her.

She'd truly believed she loved Adrian, and that he loved her. But she'd never felt anything like this in his arms. If she'd been right, then this voluptuous desire wasn't—*couldn't be*—love.

If she'd been wrong...

No, she wasn't going there. Loving Nick was out of the question, but instinct told her she'd regret it for the rest of her life if she didn't take what fate—or destiny, or perhaps her own madness!—was offering again.

Because she wanted Nick so much she could taste the hunger, feel it blazing through her veins, melting her bones, corroding her will with sweet, mind-bending temptation.

CHAPTER SEVEN

AND if he walked out on her again Siena knew she'd cope. No longer a naïve kid, she'd take what she could with no regrets.

"No second thoughts," she said soberly. "What about you?"

And, even though she was almost certain she knew the answer, her breath locked in her throat.

"None." Nick examined her with hooded eyes, their shadowed green depths unreadable. "And this time I won't say I'm sorry and leave you. I've felt a heel about it for years."

"You can stop right there," she told him. "We were both too young for any sensible behaviour."

His mouth twisted. "Too immature in my case."

She didn't know what to expect—a passionate kiss, perhaps? Something—*anything*—to help banish the last feeble protests of her inconvenient common sense?

Instead Nick put out his hand, and when she took it his fingers closed around hers in a grip that seemed to signify much more than a way to pull her closer to him. It felt like a claim, an assertion of some sort, she thought in confusion, lowering her lashes against his glinting metallic gaze.

He used his other hand to push up her chin. "Open your eyes."

Siena's lashes fluttered apart just far enough for her to see his mouth. "Why?"

"So you know who you're kissing."

This time her lashes flew up. "I know who you are," she told him, compelled by the intensity of his gaze. His expression didn't alter, and she expanded throatily, "You're Nick, and I want you."

Raising her free hand, she curved it around the hard line of his jaw, her fingertips caressing the raw silk texture. Tempting excitement sizzled though her, seductively alluring as the sea on a summer's day.

When his mouth curled into a smile she said in a husky little voice, "And if I want to close my eyes, I will."

He laughed deep in his throat and bent his head. Shivering with delicious, almost poignant anticipation, Siena felt his breath against her lips when he said, "I asked for that."

And then his mouth claimed hers, wrenching a sigh from the very depths of her being. She had never felt so utterly safe—or so exposed. Nick's kiss seared through her, demanding not just surrender but commitment, a complete yielding of herself, of everything she was and could be.

A kind of panic struggled to make itself felt, then died as a flood of pleasure overwhelmed her.

He broke the kiss, and stooped to pick her up. Her eyes opened; she gave him a look she knew had to be dazzled and dreamy, but her voice was slightly astringent when she said, "I can walk."

"Allow me my fantasies," he said on a smile that held no humour, and kissed any idea of an answer away.

Siena was so lost in delight that he'd lowered her onto the bed before she swam free of her honeyed, erotic daze and looked wildly around while he turned out the lights, leaving only one lamp to glow softly beside the bed.

Her room. Someone had pulled the sheets back ready for the night, and the linen was cool against the fevered skin of her arms and legs. She kicked off her shoes, hearing them fall to the floor with quiet thuds.

Nick sat down beside her, tanned skin drawn over the powerful framework of his face, his green eyes almost black. Gently he touched her throat, letting his fingertip linger across the skin there. Sinuous rills of exquisite sensation travelled from the point of contact to the pit of her stomach.

He asked in an oddly rough tone, "How does this pretty dress come off?"

"Over my head." Instead of in her normal voice the words came out in a gruff little mutter.

When he expertly eased the soft material over her head, she wondered with a pang how many previous lovers he'd had to gain such ease and skill.

But he'd always been deft and sure in his movements…

Although the air conditioning kept the suite at a comfortable temperature, she was shivering when the blue frock whispered from her shoulders and landed on the chair.

Nick's eyes kindled as they took in her lacy bra and narrow thong. Harshly he asked, "Cold?"

She shook her head so vigorously her black curls flew around her face. "Don't be silly."

His brows lifted and he made no attempt to touch her. "Shy?"

"A bit," she said unevenly, unable to hold his gaze.

"Why? You must know you're beautifully made."

Colour bloomed through her, and she muttered, "Thank you. I know it's stupid, but I just feel very bare right now."

He wound a curl around his finger, brushing the silken skin beneath her ear. More voluptuous little shivers rippled across her skin and right through to her heart's core.

"It's not stupid. I find it rather endearing." Smiling, he bent to kiss the thudding hollow in her throat.

Her heart leapt like a kite tossed in the wind.

Straightening, he said, "You might feel less self-conscious if I even things up."

He undid his shirt, tossing it casually on a chair across the room.

Siena's breath tore roughly from her lungs. He was outrageously magnificent, dark hair forming an antique pattern across his chest before arrowing towards the waistband of his trousers.

Her mouth dried, and she could say nothing until the lengthening silence became filled with too much meaning to be endured.

Then she swallowed and breathed, "You are— overwhelming."

Nick's chest rose and fell, and his lashes drooped. "I won't hurt you," he said abruptly.

Shocked, she said the first thing that came into her head. "I know that."

His face relaxed a little, but the look he gave her was disconcertingly keen. "Sure?"

"Absolutely."

After another assessing scrutiny he shucked his shoes, stripped off his trousers and came down beside her. In the warm golden light from the lamp his boldly chiselled face was set in uniquely male lines, dynamic and compelling.

With a shaking forefinger Siena stroked along the swell of one shoulder, then slid her palm down to that intriguing line of hair. His skin was as hot as hers, and matte, like the very finest suede.

Torn by conflicting emotions—that disconcerting shyness and a fierce relief—Siena tried to persuade her taut body to relax. Heat and the faint tang of his skin mingled to set her senses on fire. "You smell *so* good," she murmured.

Potent male…

"I was about to say the same thing." He dropped another kiss on her throat. "Do you wear perfume, or is that your natural scent?"

"It's freesia perfume," she croaked.

That was all she could manage. Nick's smoky

gaze was doing distracting things to her, summoning that fever in her blood again, stirring her emotions to a desperately reckless wildness that had her quivering inside.

His tormenting, carnal mouth moved the length of her throat, pausing when the last kiss reached the slight swell of her breast. Against the bare skin he said, "No freesia I've ever smelt has perfume like that—pure Siena, warm and delicious, and sexy as hell..."

He had to be able to hear the thunder of her heart. It was deafening her, and his words—each one an openly sensuous kiss so light she could barely feel it—robbed her limbs of their little remaining strength. When he ran a finger beneath the strap of her bra she stopped fighting and surrendered to the need that clamoured inside her.

Against her skin he murmured, "I'd like this to go too."

She nodded, holding her breath until it was efficiently removed.

Nick looked down at the gentle curves he'd revealed. His eyes darkened and he said in a voice as rough as sandpaper, "You are exquisite."

Lost in a haze of desire, Siena went under. She arched into his kiss, her body urgent and pleading, and Nick's arms tightened around her, bringing her against his lean hips so that she felt the full, vehement thrust of his male energy against her most sensitive part.

Siena gasped for breath, then released a long, half-sobbing moan. His mouth took hers again, delving deep into her sweet depths, transmuting desire into the fierce intensity she craved.

He lifted his head and almost soundlessly said, "Do you want *this*?"

All she could think of was to repeat his assertion on the dance floor. "I *want*."

She shuddered with excitement and pleasure when his lips traced a path to her breast before closing over the eager, burgeoning tip.

Nick slid his hands down to cup her breasts and, too soon, further on again to her narrow waist. His touch was sure and gentle; some taut inner part of her began to relax, letting her enjoy with sensuous pleasure his slow, confident exploration of her body.

And then he pushed her remaining garment down, and further down, until it was peeled away from her.

Enraptured by the progress of those knowing fingers, Siena forced her eyes to stay open. Without volition, her hand splayed out across his chest, pale against the iron muscles there. Awe filled her when she felt them flex against her palm.

Delicately he probed, found the centre of her desire. Her breath quickened.

His touch was like an explosion, a sunburst of sensation that swirled through her, brilliant and unbearably good, and much—too much—more than she could cope with.

"Nick..."

The word came out softly on a sigh, the merest breath of delight and anticipation, echoing her unspoken conviction that she could let herself go with him wherever he took her.

With Nick she felt utterly safe.

Safe? As though that small, unromantic word was some sort of precious talisman, her body arched into a bow when the first wave of ecstasy broke through her. Her hands clenched on him, eagerly demanding, and she cried out, wondering and triumphant while she rode those waves until they eased, leaving her dreamy and lax in his arms.

"I didn't know," she whispered, still lost to everything but the fading transcendent delight that held her prisoner.

Nick bent a searching look onto her face. In a raw voice he demanded, "Is this your first orgasm?"

Turning her head into his chest, she fought a strange reluctance to answer.

He lifted her chin and searched her flushed face with glittering eyes. "Tell me, Siena," he insisted, with formidable determination.

"Yes," she whispered finally.

Siena didn't expand; five years before he hadn't realised she was a virgin and he'd been angry afterwards. Nothing since then had compared to the rapture she'd just felt.

He said nothing for a few seconds. Secure in his arms, she mourned as the rapture sank into a delicious, lazily sensuous aftermath.

"How do you feel now?" he asked.

Pulling away, she risked a glance at his face. It revealed nothing, the expressionless mask firmly back in place.

Chilled, she said, "Good. I mean, great." *Calm down,* she ordered, and took a deep breath. "Why do you ask?"

His voice was carefully neutral. "I wondered if you'd like to stop there."

Siena looked blankly at him, but asked in her turn, "Would *you* like to?"

And held her breath until he said, "No."

"Oh, good," she said fervently.

Nick's laughter was low and unforced. "Then we're both in agreement."

He bent his head and kissed her again, making himself master of the soft depths of her mouth.

To her rash exhilaration the smouldering embers of her desire flared into flames again.

This time it was even more...more everything, she thought, as he acquainted her with pleasure points she hadn't known existed and with skilful patience led her on a long, infinitely fulfilling path to the moment when at last he eased over her and into her.

Wide-eyed, she stared at him. He was so controlled, she thought with a frisson of unease.

"All right?" he asked quietly.

"Yes." How could he discipline his reactions like that? Hers were headstrong and intoxicating and utterly irresistible.

And why was he asking? Surely he understood by now that she was neither fragile nor the inexperienced virgin he'd taken so long ago?

At last he moved again, muscles flowing as he pushed further, easing into her with such subtlety that she could have screamed with delicious, erotic satisfaction when finally he took full possession.

Wild appetite rioted through her, tightening

every nerve in her body. She made an odd little noise—half-grunt, half-plea—and allowed sensation to vanquish her completely until she realised he was about to withdraw. Instinctively she clenched her inner muscles.

"It's all right," he soothed, and slid his arms beneath her shoulders to support himself on his elbows. He looked down at her and his mouth curved in a faint, humourless smile. "There—is that what you want?"

Slowly, almost gently, he moved again, and Siena said on a long, indrawn breath, "Oh, yes, *please*..." letting the words trail away in a sigh of sheer delight.

She could feel his leashed strength, the almost violent command he was exerting over himself, and again wondered if he was afraid he might hurt her. The thought was unbearable.

Gripped by that savage, demanding tension, she arched into him again. Although he resisted her voiceless plea, almost immediately his control snapped, and he thrust as though he would never get enough of her.

The desperate, primal hunger rioting through Siena welcomed and matched his unrestrained passion. Now that she knew what lay ahead she gave herself up to the waves of exquisite sensation until at last she reached that other dimension where rapture was all she could feel—a rapture that ravished the thoughts from her mind and hurled her into a sated, almost stunned oblivion.

Nick immediately followed her into that place; his climax gave depth to her own, and together they rode the storm until at last it eased into blissful fulfilment.

Siena said, "No!" when he rolled over onto his side, but he ignored her and scooped her so that she came to rest stretched out on top of him.

"All right?" he asked, his voice rough.

"So very all right," she said huskily into his shoulder, and bit his skin there, relishing the salt tang of it, the musky male flavour. "Actually, I don't think I've ever felt better."

As soon as she said the words she wished she hadn't. The first time they'd made love had been wonderful but there had been pain, and she hadn't reached the earth-shaking peak she'd just experienced.

Now, she thought with an odd sinking feeling in the region of her heart, *now* she knew.

And she'd never be the same again.

In Nick's arms she'd been utterly transported into a new and different dimension, where the only thing that mattered was the sensation he summoned from her unaware body.

But it had been stupid—and dangerous—to let him see that. Although with his experience he'd probably have recognised her wild behaviour for what it was—a primitive, unthinking pleasure so entirely new to her she couldn't check or hide her emotions.

Perhaps she should have tried for the casual sophistication he no doubt expected from his lovers. It wouldn't have worked; she'd been so lost in the moment she'd been unable to fake anything at all.

"I didn't realise you were—" he paused, before finishing abruptly "—unawakened. I must have been damned clumsy that first time."

His tone was so flat she didn't know what he was thinking. Or feeling. Regret for not sticking to friendship? Was he—oh, horrors!—concerned about how this would affect her parents? She cringed at the thought.

Worse still, had her passionate response made him warily wonder if she might be falling in love with him?

That last humiliating thought made up her mind. Cheerful insouciance—that was what he was used to from her, so that was what she'd give him now.

"It's no big deal," she said, hoping she sounded properly free and easy. "And, no, you weren't clumsy. It was—great. All and more than I hoped for. Just not as great as this time."

His face still sombre, he said, "I felt like a roué after that. I was furious with myself for not realising you were a virgin."

"Nick, it's all right. According to my friends and every woman's magazine I've ever read it's far from uncommon." She met his eyes and managed a smile. "I should be thanking you for showing me there's a lot more to this sex business than simple pleasure."

Not a muscle in his big body moved. A twist of something strangely like fear raked through her at the glittering sliver of green beneath his lashes.

And then he smiled, and she should have been able to relax. "Oh, you haven't learnt anything yet," he drawled. "With a little encouragement I can do so much better than that."

She stiffened, and his arm tightened around her—not in threat, but certainly with the unspoken implication that she was there until he chose to let her go.

"You're angry," she blurted.

"And you're perceptive."

It wasn't a sneer, but it came too close. "Not very," she said, steadying her voice, "because I don't have the faintest idea of what's made you angry."

To her intense relief he laughed with real humour. Her intimation of an oncoming storm was so completely banished she could almost convince herself she'd misread the situation.

He let her go, but only to cup his hands around the sides of her face and bring her head down until their mouths were separated by nothing more than a whisper of air.

Hers was warmed with his breath when he murmured, "Forget it. You must remember that I can be moody."

"I don't—" But her refutation was kissed into oblivion.

Soon seduced into surrender, she sighed and gave herself to him.

Much later, alone in the big bed, she wondered. It hadn't been an empty boast when he'd said he could do better, but now she was no longer lost along the wilder shores of passionate ecstasy she wished he hadn't been in such complete control, playing her like a virtuoso.

Uneasily she moved, feeling the slight tug of muscles unaccustomed to the exercise they'd endured. It was almost as though he'd been proving something.

To her? She drew in a breath and let it sigh out again. Presumably.

So why did she have the weird feeling he might actually be trying to prove that mysterious something to himself? He'd always been so self-contained, even when he was a serious twelve-year-old. At first, with the innocence of childhood, she'd believed he didn't like their family. It was only later she'd realised that his cool self-discipline was armour.

Against what?

She'd never known—never would know. Just as she would never understand what went on in his brilliant brain, rarely be able to identify the emotions he hid so successfully.

However, she *did* understand that he was probably regretting the change in their relationship to lovers.

And *lovers* was the wrong word, she thought, gripped by a stabbing regret. This was a one-night stand, not a love affair. Not even an affair.

One day she might be able to truly be grateful

to him for showing her how incandescent love-making could be.

Tears clogged her eyes, and she turned over and tried desperately to summon some innocuous thoughts that would let her woo sleep.

Nick stared at his newly shaven face, cursing silently and at length. He had a long day—an important day—ahead of him, and he needed every brain cell he possessed.

Unfortunately far too many of them were occupied with processing voluptuous memories of the previous night. He'd barely slept, and now wherever he looked he seemed to register only Siena's delicious shock at her first complete orgasm.

Not her last, he thought with unwelcome satisfaction, before swearing out loud and turning away from the mirror. Of course he couldn't indulge in an affair with her. She was on the rebound from what had clearly been an unsatisfactory relationship—sexually, anyway, and probably in other ways.

And the fact that her fiancé had chosen Gemma over her wouldn't be helping.

He should never have made love to her. God, only on the plane he'd vowed not to touch her again—a resolution he'd abandoned the minute he'd succumbed to temptation and asked her to dance.

Grimacing, he turned away from the mirror. Somehow she had power over him—an innocent power, because she didn't recognise it. Even if she had, it wouldn't be important to her.

He recalled his swift, shattering fury when she'd made it clear she regarded him as nothing more than a means to an end.

"I should be thanking you for showing me there's a lot more to this sex business than simple pleasure..."

Possibly, he thought with black humour, he was the one who needed to discard illusions.

Had she really loved the idiot who hadn't even noticed that he didn't turn her on?

And what was she going to do when she arrived back in Auckland?

Any sensible man would send her off in the jet this morning by herself. He swore again, but even as he went out to eat breakfast with Siena he knew he'd be going to New Zealand with her.

Of course she was already up, looking fresh and unaffected by their torrid night together, although the smile and greeting she bestowed on him were a little forced.

He should have been relieved. He was not.

"I'm looking forward to the museum," she told him chattily. "Is this an all-day meeting you're embarking on?"

His broad shoulders lifted slightly. "No. We've been talking for months, and yesterday negotiations started in earnest. It won't get to any signatures yet, but there will be a statement for the press, and a resolution to continue talks. In this part of the world everything takes time and you need to establish trust."

She gave him a speculative look. "Do you enjoy it still? I can see that at the beginning there'd have been enormous excitement and stimulation in setting everything up and watching it begin to grow, but how about now? Do you still feel the same elation?"

Nobody had ever asked Nick that before. He knew she noted his surprise, and said with more frankness than he had intended, "Mostly. And people's livelihoods rely on me getting the job done."

"I suppose it's a bit like having a child," she said thoughtfully. "Once you've made the decision to have one, you have to look after it until it's old enough to care for itself. You can't just abandon it. Anyone who sets up an organisation must feel the same way."

"Some parents have no difficulty in abandoning their children, emotionally if not physically," he said cynically. And some were forced to—his own mother for one.

A thought struck him. "I hope you're not trying to suggest there's a possibility—?"

Colour flaring through her exquisite skin, she broke in hotly, "Of course not! Really, Nick, I'm not an idiot! Just as I'm prepared to bet you're not going to inform me now you've got some vile disease!"

For the first time that morning Nick laughed. "I don't, so you can relax."

"I don't need to relax because I knew perfectly well you wouldn't have—I mean, we wouldn't have made love if you had..." Her voice tailed away and colour pinked her silky skin.

He was surprised and oddly elated by her declaration, but his voice was hard when he said, "You should never take anything so important on trust."

"Nick, I *know* you. Or are you trying to tell me that no woman can trust any man?"

"Probably." He glanced at his watch. "I have to go. Enjoy your day."

"You too."

But he was conscious of her gaze on him as he left the suite, and spent a few minutes wondering just what she was thinking before forcibly changing the direction of his thoughts to the negotiations ahead.

CHAPTER EIGHT

WHEN she heard Nick arrive back at the suite Siena tensed, but pride and a strong sense of self-preservation stopped her from turning to greet him in case her radiant face gave her away.

It was just as well. In a cool, uninvolved tone he said, "Everything packed?"

"Yes." Of course she hadn't expected anything like joy at the sight of her, but even a mild plea-sure would be better than this dampening neu-trality.

No, she corrected herself, it would not. Mild pleasure would be *insulting*. And nothing had changed; when had she ever seen Nick unable to master his emotions?

But as they went through the final formalities of leaving she found herself wondering just what was going on behind the handsome, arrogant mask of his features. What *was* he feeling?

Regret, possibly. He might even be wondering how on earth he'd managed to get himself into this situation…

No, not Nick. He always knew exactly what he was doing.

In the car on the way to the airport he asked, "Have you let your sister know you're coming home early?"

"No." Shamed, she realised she'd barely thought of Gemma these past few days.

When he didn't answer she enlarged, "She'll still be in Australia. Why do you ask? I'll catch a shuttle from the airport—"

"Don't be silly. I'll take you," he said curtly. "Where are you living now?"

"When I gave up my job I also gave up my flat. While Mum and Dad are away I'm staying at their place. If Gemma's back in New Zealand she'll be there too."

He nodded. "No problem, then."

After a second's hesitation Siena said, "Well—

thank you," and turned to fix her gaze on the view outside the big car.

With an odd pang of foreboding she realised Hong Kong would always hold a special place in her heart, because here she'd discovered the power and intensity of her own sexuality.

She looked down at her hands, knotted together in her lap. Hastily forcing them apart, she fixed her unseeing gaze on the teeming streets outside.

Hong Kong was also where she'd finally accepted her real feelings for Nick. Her stomach tightened as though warding off a blow, but she forced herself to articulate the words she'd hidden from for so long.

She loved him.

She loved Nicholas Grenville.

She'd always loved him—certainly before they'd first made love.

A heavy weight settled on her chest, shortening her breath as the full impact of her discovery hit her.

How on earth could you love someone and not know it?

Thoughts churned through her head, bewildering and jumbled. Actually, she always known, but in a faint-hearted effort to protect herself she'd refused to acknowledge her deepest feelings.

Because she'd always known they were doomed. Nick wouldn't allow himself to love.

That was why she'd settled for a safe, unthreatening relationship with Adrian. Now she understood why his defection hadn't hurt as much as it should. Almost certainly, she thought with remorse, he'd sensed her ambivalence, a distance she hadn't known she'd felt.

No wonder he'd fallen in love with Gemma.

Keeping her gaze fixed through the window, she fought back her cold panic by working out what to do next.

First face reality, she told herself sternly. Although she loved Nick, she'd always sensed he didn't—possibly *couldn't*—return her love, and what she'd read of his affairs had reinforced that instinctive knowledge.

If he suggested an affair, what on earth would she do?

Her chin came up as she fought the slow creep of despair. Wanting more from him than he could give was not only futile, it was stupid and unfair. Nick had made no promises and demanded nothing from her.

An affair would only reinforce this desperate unreturned love. Although the prospect cut her to the heart, she knew a quick clean break would be the least painful way to end this—this passionate interlude.

Of course he might not want anything more from her.

But if he did…? Did she have the courage to turn him down?

Or should she surrender to her wildest urgings, take what she could from him and then live on memories for the rest of her life?

"That's a very determined look," Nick said, his idle tone at variance with his keen scrutiny. "Plotting something?"

Siena's mind raced. "Getting back in touch with real life." Hoping she didn't sound too glib, she added with a shrug, "I should be working out tactics for landing a good job."

"Any ideas?"

"Not a lot right now, because I'm still in holiday mode," she said briskly. "Once I get back home I'll apply myself to finding something that involves plants. One of the reasons I enjoyed working at the nursery was because I could help now and then with ideas for people who were planning their gardens."

"Perhaps you should have taken that landscaping course," he said without emphasis. "Although a commerce degree would help if you do decide to go that way. You'll do well whatever you choose. I can't recall an instance when you didn't reach a goal you'd set your mind on."

Her brows shot up. "What about the extra six inches in height I yearned for when I was fifteen?"

A lazily amused smile curled his mouth. "I'm sure you knew it was never going to happen by then and were far too sensible to repine. Anyway, I can't imagine you tall."

Siena's wayward mind inconveniently flew to the complete security she'd felt when he carried her into the bedroom. Colour heated the sweep of her cheekbones.

His eyes narrowed, and for a heart-shattering second she wondered if he too was remembering. It was a relief when the car stopped.

"Oh, we're here," she said inanely. She felt as though she'd refused to take a chance, one that would never to be repeated—that something precious was lost to her forever.

That wistful sense of loss stayed with her all through the flight.

They landed in the middle of a glorious night in Auckland. The city's notoriously fickle climate had turned on ideal weather to welcome her home, Siena thought bleakly as she watched the lights shimmer golden around the shores of the harbour, the decorated symmetry of the Sky Tower an emphatic exclamation point in the downtown area.

The bustle of landing provided a charge of

adrenalin, but it soon dissipated, and once she was safely ensconced in the car that had met them she leaned back and closed her eyes, far too conscious of the man who sat silently beside her.

It seemed to take for ever to reach her parents' home, and she was rather tense when the car that had met them drew to a stop.

Opening her eyes, she stared through the window at the forecourt, then turned an astonished face to Nick. "This isn't—"

"We're at my house," he said calmly.

She opened her mouth to ask why, then remembered the driver. Fortunately he got out and opened the boot, giving her the chance to demand, "What's going on?"

"It's all right," Nick said.

Dumbly she watched him get out and walk around the car to open her door. When she didn't move, he reached in, took her hand and helped her out rather more forcefully than necessary.

She blinked as he let her go and turned to pick up her bag.

"Come on." His tone was clipped, almost curt.

Later she'd think she had to be suffering some insidious form of jet-lag, because she obediently followed him into the house, dimly conscious of soft scents from his garden and the gentle hush of waves against the beach below.

But once inside she listened to the car drawing away and took a deep breath. Losing her temper wasn't going to help. "Why did you bring me here?" she asked, almost temperately.

"Gemma's back," he said in an edged voice. "Did you really want to go to your parents' place right now?"

"How do you know?"

"I rang from the airport."

She shook her head, trying to clear it. "It was my decision to make, not yours."

"In other words," he said smoothly, his tone ironic, "you're glad I made it for you."

The knowledge that he was right, that he must have seen straight through her bravado made her lash out. "Has anyone ever told you you're a high-handed, bossy, domineering—"

"Stop right there."

Startled at the curt note in his words, she stared at him.

He gave her a hard half-smile, with an edge of self-mockery. "Dominating I'll accept, but I'm not domineering and you know it."

Her already strained nerves twanged like guitar strings. "I can't stay with you."

"Have you got a better idea?" he asked, more seriously. "You're probably jet-lagged and in no fit state to talk to your sister now. If I know Gemma she'll weep all over you and you'll spend the night trying to comfort her. Stop being so staunch and give yourself a decent night's sleep and a chance to draw breath before you tackle her."

He was right; exhaustion had sapped her strength, rendering both body and mind sluggish. Too much had happened in the past few days, and she was assailed by a bone-deep lethargy that demanded at least ten hours of oblivion.

Stubbornly she reiterated, "You shouldn't have made the decision for me."

He said impatiently, "All right, then, I shouldn't. Now will you stop protesting?"

Reluctantly yielding, she said, "Dominating is definitely correct. Just don't think you can keep on doing it."

He picked up her pack and gave her a coolly speculative smile. "Come on, we'll make up a bed for you. You look as though you've been through a wringer, and I could do with a few hours' uninterrupted sleep myself."

As a rejection it was tactful, but very clear. And it hurt. Love shouldn't hurt, she thought sombrely.

The sooner she was out of here the better, but a sluggish inertia silenced her. Tomorrow, she promised herself—tomorrow she'd be able to deal with everything. Right then she craved sleep.

Although Nick no longer spent much time in New Zealand, his house had none of the forlorn air of a place without inhabitants. A faint scent of lavender polish permeated the air, and on the hall table a large vase was radiant with summer flowers—roses, lushly opulent peonies from the

South Island, and long scented stems of mock orange blossom, skilfully arranged.

Rallying her chaotic thoughts into order, she flicked an upward glance and looked away again, hardly giving herself time to appreciate the arrogantly sculpted features that matched the aura of power Nick radiated.

Fair-haired and blue-eyed, Adrian was conventionally handsome, but Nick's bold face and lithe strength were supported and enhanced by an effortless presence that marked him out from other men. One glance was all it took to make his rapid rise entirely credible.

At nineteen, armed with courage, tenacity and complete confidence in his own ability, he'd parlayed a brilliant idea into a huge internet success. Since then he'd gone from strength to strength, yet he'd never been seduced by either fame or fortune.

"You can sleep in here," he said, opening a door. "I'll get sheets and towels."

He put the pack down on a chair and went out. Siena looked around the room, barely taking in its quiet, sophisticated charm. Struggling to control a bewildering jumble of emotions, she took refuge in action, pulling the covers from the bed.

Only a few more minutes, she promised herself. *Hold on for a few more minutes—and then you can let go.*

She seemed to have said that more than a few times recently.

When Nick came back she said, "Thanks. I can do this now."

"I'll help you."

She said unevenly, "I'd rather you didn't."

He dumped the sheets on the bed and straightened. "Siena, look at me."

The last time he'd said that... *No,* she wasn't going to let memories of their lovemaking overwhelm her. Shivers scudded the length of her spine, but she met his probing green scrutiny without flinching.

"All right," he said eventually. "I'll see you in the morning. Sleep well."

Siena watched him leave, waiting until the door had closed firmly before wandering across the room. Coming to a halt in front of the dressing table, she peered at her reflection in the mirror with dull eyes.

How could a few days create such turmoil in her life, turning it completely upside down, forcing her to reassess everything she'd done over the past few years?

She hadn't loved Adrian, not as he should be loved. Not as Gemma so clearly did…

They'd been good friends before they'd become engaged, and she'd valued him for his honesty and his strength of character. She'd been happy when he'd proposed. Oh, she'd known it wasn't the sort of fantasy love she'd read about in books, all trumpet calls and romantic music and soaring to the stars, but she'd not been looking for that.

And now she understood why.

Her mouth twisted into a small, bitter smile. Adrian had been a safe refuge, because long before she'd met him her heart had been given to Nick. It had escaped her control and surrendered to a man who'd never want it.

She turned away and made the bed, then went

through her nightly routine, but the sleep she so ardently wooed refused to come. After hearing a distant clock chime midnight she got up and pulled a light T-shirt and her jeans on over her pyjamas. If she didn't walk off the thoughts that continually forced themselves on her she'd go mad.

No such luck, she thought dismally as she slipped out of the door onto the terrace outside. Anyway, going mad wouldn't help. Somehow, no matter how difficult it was, she'd have to find a way of dealing with her forlorn love.

But right now she needed fresh air.

She stood a moment, squinting until her eyes adjusted to the darkness. Unseen except for the glow in the sky to the west, the city slept in silence.

Siena dragged in a deep, deep breath. Exquisite, exotic perfume drifted on the warm air from the huge white-velvet trumpet of datura hanging beneath an umbrella of large leaves, and the full moon turned the harbour into silver and black silk beneath the Milky Way, a girdle of diamonds across the indigo velvet sky. When she turned her head she saw the Southern Cross, a glittering pendant pointing southwards.

Yet the peace she longed for evaded her. Making up her mind, she walked towards the cliff edge. Somewhere beneath the huge old trees a flight of steps led down to a small cove of white sand. She'd like to run for miles, run herself into exhaustion, but a walk along the little beach to the sleepy sibilance of the wavelets might help calm the turbulence of her mind.

At the top of the cliff a small summerhouse had been built for Nick's mother, carefully positioned to catch the summer dawn through the huge boughs of a sprawling sentinel pohutukawa. Darkly shaded, both tree and summerhouse looked almost sinister now. Telling herself not to be foolish, Siena stopped at the top of the flight of steps to peer down. As she'd guessed, the moon showed each level with perfect clarity and, just to make sure no one fell, a handrail bordered the steps on the seaward side.

Without warning, she was grabbed from behind

and hauled backwards. Wide-eyed and terrified, she opened her mouth but her scream was cut short by a hard hand. She struggled wildly in an unrelenting grip, shocked by the ruthless strength of the man who'd overpowered her.

"Stop it, Siena." Nick's hard voice came like a shower of cold water.

Her terror was transformed into fury and relief. She went rigid, whispering against his palm, "Let me go," and sagged back against him when he dragged her back from the edge of the cliff.

But he still didn't let her go. Panting, she twisted futilely in his grip until he dropped the hand across her mouth and turned her.

She closed her eyes, then forced them open again, still unable to believe what had happened. Glaring up into his face, its strong framework emphasised by moonlight, she demanded hoarsely, "What on earth are you doing?"

Nick loosened his grip further. Relief surged through her—closely followed by a lick of heat that sent another shockwave along her nerves.

Siena fought back the impulse to taste the indefinable sexy flavour lingering on her lips. It fired her senses and sent another unstoppable shiver through her.

Mind whirling, she tried to step away. For a terrifying heartbeat she'd thought she was being attacked—and she was, but the assault came from within, a heady response that refused to be ignored.

Nick had only to touch her and she wanted him.

It took a massive effort of will to control the sensuous effect his clean male taste was still wreaking on her body and brain. Her chest expanded, dragging air into her famished lungs.

Instantly his mouth covered hers, stopping any words with a kiss that sent her blood rocketing through her body and banished every thought from her brain in a flood of shameless pleasure.

It was over too soon.

No, too late.

Too late because when he lifted his mouth she ached with emptiness. Slowly she raised heavy eyelids, peeping through lashes that had somehow drifted down while he was kissing her. It seemed to take ages for her star-dazzled eyes to adjust enough to make out the strongly marked features and the angular line of his jaw, the sensual curve of his mouth.

Heat from that intoxicating hunger still lingered in every cell, transforming her from a woman in command of her life to an astonished, witless stranger.

"What the hell were you doing?" Nick demanded beneath his breath.

She dragged in a sudden sharp breath. "I needed some fresh air. I was going down to the beach."

He seemed to relax, but his eyes never left her face while he said harshly, "From where I stood it looked as though you'd chosen the quick way to get down there."

When she stared at him in bewilderment, he added, "By throwing yourself over."

"No!"

Swallowing, she tore her gaze away from Nick's eyes, darkly unreadable in the bold contours of his face.

His arms around her tightened, forcing her

against his lean, powerful body. The renewed contact stirred that dismaying, disruptive heat into flames again.

Siena's throat muscles locked.

In a voice pitched so low she had to struggle to hear him, Nick said, "I'm sorry I gave you such a fright, but, *hell*—for a stupid moment I thought you'd decided to take the easy way out of this damned imbroglio."

She drew in a shaking, hard-won breath. "You should know me better than that."

"I do."

Siena opened her mouth to speak, only to have the words crushed by the renewed pressure of Nick's mouth. Astounded, she struggled against the drugging sensuousness his kiss provoked.

Nicholas broke the carnal spell by lifting his head. "Come on, let's get out of here. I need a drink."

Vainly Siena tried to rally common sense and fortitude. "But—"

"But what?" Nick's tone was back to his trademark cool neutrality.

Mouth tautly controlled, she angled her chin. She couldn't discern any emotion in his handsome face, and in the scented stillness they measured glances like swordsmen determining the perfect moment to attack.

Until she asked, "What on earth made you think I'd be likely to try and kill myself?"

He released her and, startled, she staggered a little. Instantly he steadied her.

"I didn't—I don't," he corrected bluntly. "But you looked—lost. As though your life had collapsed around you."

Struggling to regain some composure, she swallowed before managing to say in what sounded almost like her normal voice, "Even if it had, I wouldn't do that."

"I realise that now," he said curtly. "In fact, I knew then—it was a reflex action, nothing more. Do you still want to walk?"

"I've got a fair amount of adrenalin churning through me. Can you—?" She stopped just in time to hold back the words *Can you think of a better way to use it up?*

Unfortunately she could, but clearly Nick was in no mood to make love. Ever since they'd got up in Hong Kong he'd been withdrawing. Oh, it wasn't as brutal as the first time he'd walked out on her, but she knew rejection when she experienced it.

So what about those kisses a few minutes ago?

Relief? Or perhaps a subtle punishment? As soon as she'd responded he'd released her.

"All right, then, let's get down there." He strode off towards the steps that snaked down the cliff-face.

Still shaken, Siena followed.

The little bay was no more than a cove, and they walked in silence along the yielding white sand for some minutes before he asked conversationally, "Were you in love with him?"

Were, she noticed. Her heart twisted. Had she ever been in love with Adrian?

But the memory of the way she'd felt in Nick's arms overshadowed everything else. Her mouth dried.

In a way she'd betrayed Adrian.

"I certainly believed I was," she said in gruff voice.

"It's trite to say it, but it's not the end of the world."

She sent him a level glance. He was tough and dominant, brilliant and quick to make up his mind, utterly determined, master of his life.

No doubt he could move from one relationship to another without tearing himself to pieces.

Siena's jagged breath hurt, but her voice was composed and crisp when she answered, "I know that. Have you ever been in love?"

And wondered at her own effrontery.

Nick paused, then admitted curtly, "Yes."

Who? she thought, savaged by a lethal jealousy. Which of the several women linked romantically to him had been the one?

Pain sawed through her, so intense she couldn't speak. It served her right for being so nosy.

Nick said, "What are your plans now?"

She watched the romantic moon veil itself in a faint wisp of cloud. Reaching deep inside herself, she said quietly, "You were right when you said

I needed a decent night's sleep." Although right now that seemed a forlorn hope. "Tomorrow I'll work out what to do."

"Any ideas?"

She hesitated, then said quietly, "I don't know yet." And added in a much stronger voice, "But don't you dare feel sorry for me, and for heaven's sake don't think I'm going to do something stupid. I'll manage."

"Spoken like a survivor." The flash of strong white teeth revealed a humourless smile.

"I am a survivor," she said, and left it at that, looking away from his too-perceptive survey.

Nick glanced down. Hadn't she suspected Worth at all?

No, he thought savagely, she hadn't. She'd trusted that idiot completely.

His body stirred at the memory of how she felt in his arms. Repressing that spontaneous and inconvenient reaction, he wondered how she'd deal with the situation.

That she *would* deal with it was a given—she had guts and strength—but another swift glance revealed that her mouth was held in a taut line in her strained face.

What the hell was she thinking? How did she feel about their lovemaking? Since waking that morning she'd been studiously casual, as though it meant nothing more than a pleasant interlude. Perhaps to her it didn't.

With sardonic amusement at his own contrariness, he knew that if she'd been any other woman he'd have welcomed her attitude.

Instead it roused a possessiveness he despised. He wanted to physically shake her into awareness of him.

When she frowned he said, "I'm sorry for frightening you."

He let that hang in the air, and eventually she said with a wry smile, "And I'm sorry you found yourself in the middle of a family drama. Actually, being grabbed did startle me, but I've done martial arts training and I think I could have taken you out."

His brows shot up. "How?"

"I'd have gone for your eyes," she told him

nonchalantly. "They're usually the least expected target. And when you're as short as I am, and with curly hair, most people expect you to scream and struggle foolishly instead of fighting back."

Nicholas cast another incredulous glance her way, then laughed, but he sobered when he said, "Confidence is good, but too much can hinder."

A fierce protectiveness stirred in him. She did look younger than her twenty-four years, but he wondered how many other people had made the mistake of judging her on height alone.

And close on that thought came other questions: had she ever had to use her skill? Had she studied martial arts because she'd been a target?

Possibly the now ex-employer, he thought, controlling with surprising difficulty a swift surge of cold anger.

Obviously she was able to look after herself. The shock value alone of her training would startle most men into a reaction that would give her an advantage.

However, sometimes a knowledge of martial arts gave people a false idea of their ability to deal with situations. Abruptly he said, "Whatever form of art you studied, always remember your size is a disadvantage."

"I know that. My first line of attack is to keep away from situations that might lead to problems."

"And your second?"

Siena managed a grin. "Scream like crazy and run. So far I haven't had to use that one."

Another considering glance revealed a relaxed mouth, but it was impossible to tell from her expression what was going on beneath her black curls.

Nick had no illusions about her response to him. A mixture of desperation and the cruel shock of rejection had driven her into his arms. The fact that he'd been able to bring her to unexpected orgasm had been an accidental bonus for her.

And she certainly didn't expect anything further from him.

Her curls were fastened back from her face, but one had escaped to lie artlessly curled in the hollow of her throat. He resisted an impulse to brush it away and let his fingers trail across the pulse that beat rapidly beneath.

She was a cool one, yet fire lurked beneath that restraint. The strength and heat of her ardour kicked off an impressively fierce hunger in him—a hunger that still burned like fire in the pit of his belly whenever he looked at her.

Siena flicked back the straying lock with a casual toss of her head and looked up, those amazing blue eyes direct as they met his. She said quietly, "First I have to find a job."

But for now she would walk in the moonlight with him, the whispering waves a serene background, and forever hold every sight, every sound, the piercing pleasure of his presence, in her heart.

CHAPTER NINE

NICK was woken early by an important telephone call from New York. He dealt with it swiftly, then lay back against the pillows and frowned at the dawn sky.

Five years previously he'd vowed never to hurt another woman. Since then he'd steered well away from emotional entanglements, choosing sophisticated lovers who knew the rules, who understood and accepted that while a relationship with him would involve fidelity until it ended, it wouldn't lead to commitment. It had earned him a reputation for coldness, but that was better than breaking hearts.

And Siena was no longer inexperienced. She'd had at least one other lover. Besides, the sexual connection between them was even more powerful. His body tightened when he recalled her consuming, incandescent response, and her wondering joy when she'd finally reached her peak in his arms.

However, although the sex might have been a revelation to her, it was based on her longing for comfort and reassurance. He'd shown her with his passion that she was infinitely desirable, and helped restore her faith in herself.

So why the hell was he lying here in his own bed instead of waking up beside her?

Because, although Siena wasn't in love with him, she was still on the rebound from her ex-fiancé. And for some unfathomable reason Nick wanted more from her than lust on the rebound.

Swearing silently, he rolled over and looked at the alarm clock. She'd still be asleep. Last night she'd been completely exhausted—a tiredness he suspected was caused mostly by the prospect of dealing with the fall-out from her broken engagement.

And, because Worth had fallen for Gemma, Siena had no way of avoiding the situation.

Driven by a need for action, Nick got up, strode

across the room and pulled back the curtains, looking across the wide spread of lawn to the sea beyond. With so much travelling in his life an apartment on Auckland's waterfront would be a more practical base in New Zealand, but coming to this house was coming home, although his mother had been dead some years now. Far too young...

At least he'd been able to make sure she'd spent the last period of her life in contentment and with every comfort he could provide. She deserved that after the hell she'd endured with his father.

Even those bitter memories couldn't quench his body's blatant response to the thought of making love to Siena. He forced his brain into logic mode, totting up the things about her that appealed to him.

Her intelligence, for a start, and that mental astringency. She intrigued him because he never knew what she'd say next. Or do.

Only Siena would have donated the money she'd extracted from her ex-employer to a refuge for victims of abuse. Ruthlessly he controlled his anger. He might want to physically punish the man who'd tried to force her into sex with him, but there were other, ultimately more satisfactory ways to punish would-be rapists.

Of the women he knew, only Siena would have spent all her savings to fly to London to be with her parents on their special night.

Small, vibrant, loving and loyal, she would, he suspected, throw herself heart and soul into any relationship. That was why he'd left her five years ago. He hadn't wanted to raise false hopes, hadn't wanted to hurt her beyond the pain he'd already caused. And making love to her had roused emotions he hadn't known how to deal with.

Fear, mainly.

He tasted the word, hating it, but forced to admit its accuracy. Fear, and the overwhelming drive to prove himself.

He'd fought hard for the independence he now had, but because of that brutal battle with himself and the corrosive legacy of his father had he lost something of even greater worth?

He'd expected the hunger Siena aroused to be

temporary, a quick cheap thrill that would abate as soon as she left his arms. But once roused that erotic appetite had lodged in him, a silken claw in his self-esteem. It was still there.

Gradually his unseeing gaze focused on the scene below, registering rows of rose bushes struggling to survive in the salt air. Born and raised in the tropics, his mother had longed for an English garden.

The handyman he employed kept the beds weed-free and tidy, but apart from the pool area, which he'd had revitalised a couple of years ago, the garden lacked any connection with the magnificent seascape before him.

Inspiration hit him—one of the hunches he was noted for. Usually they were right on the mark. If this one wasn't—well, he hadn't got where he was without a certain amount of guile and a hell of a lot of persistence.

When he opened his bedroom door Siena was walking down the hall. "Good morning," he said, searching her face for signs of tiredness or strain. "How did you sleep?"

Her gaze skimmed him with insulting speed, and the smile she gave was a little less dazzling than usual. It was impossible for that milk-white skin to be even paler, but he sensed a subtle weariness in her when she said sedately, "Very well, thank you."

Strangely gratified by the hint of colour along her cheekbones before long lashes half-hid her eyes, he eyed her narrow-cut jeans and a shirt the same vivid blue as her eyes that hinted at curves he remembered well.

"Hong Kong purchases?" he guessed.

She smiled. "Grace talked me into the shirt after we'd been to the museum."

"It suits you."

"She has great taste as well as top-class bargaining skills." Lush mouth held in a firm line, she tilted her chin at an angle that could be called defiant and stated succinctly, "I need coffee."

Amazingly Siena had slept well, but only to wake long before dawn. When she'd finally been able to make out her hand in front of her face she'd got up, pulling back the curtains to gaze out over the sea to the dark bulk of Rangitoto Island, the newest of Auckland's small volcanoes. Although the sun had still been beneath the horizon nascent light had glimmered with a pearly sheen over the harbour, and above the island the morning star had shone with such radiance Siena had had to blink back a tear.

"Home again," she'd said softly, against a background of gulls calling insistently across the water.

But now apprehension knotted her stomach, backed by a burgeoning excitement when she watched Nick's brows climb, met his unsettling regard.

"You need coffee that urgently?" His voice was cool, even a little bored, although his hard green eyes scanned her face before he turned and held open a door that led, she realised, into the kitchen.

"At this time of the morning I always need coffee," she told him.

Fortunately the coffeemaker was one she could cope with, so she set it going, finding her way around the kitchen by instinct. "What are you having for breakfast?" she enquired.

"Eggs and bacon. Do you want some?"

Hastily Siena shook her head. The thought of eggs made her stomach lurch. "I'll just have toast, thanks. How is it that this place is full of fresh food when you've been away for months?"

"I emailed the agency from Hong Kong."

"Agency?"

He smiled. "I employ an agency to take care of things like stocking the kitchen whenever I come back."

"Goodness," she said, awed. "I wish I could afford someone to take care of mundane details like that!"

"Works for me." He looked around. "Why don't you set the table out on the terrace while I cook my breakfast? The sun's fully up, and it should be warm enough even after Hong Kong."

It was. In fact, it was glorious. Siena set the table, picked a bunch of white daisies from a large bush and put them in a glass tumbler, then took out her toast and sat down with a small sigh.

"It's great to be home again," she said when Nick joined her.

"Don't you like travelling?"

"I like it very much, but I'm always glad to get back. What about you?"

He gave her a quizzical glance. "Mostly it's for business, but I try to see something in each place I've never seen before."

"Being a tourist?"

He nodded. "Although I prefer to call myself a traveller."

Siena sliced a tomato and arranged the slices over her toast. "I like that," she said thoughtfully, and ate the last slice with relish. "And I love the new season's tomatoes. The new season's anything, actually. I adore asparagus, because not only does it taste delicious but it only arrives once a year."

Stop babbling, she told herself when Nick looked across at her. He could have fresh new asparagus flown to him any time he liked...

But he nodded as he expertly ladled his eggs

onto a bed of bacon and slid grilled tomatoes onto the plate. "Agreed."

Foolishly, Siena wondered why it seemed far more intimate to be eating breakfast they'd made themselves than at the table in the hotel suite.

She nibbled her suddenly tasteless toast and took a fortifying sip of coffee before saying without preamble, "Gemma contacted me last night."

Eyebrow cocked, Nick waited.

She hesitated, then went on with a trace of defiance, "She sent me a text."

One black brow climbed higher. "Full of tears and pleas, no doubt?"

Siena paused, then said reluctantly, "Yes."

"Which kept you awake most of the night, judging by the shadows under your eyes," Nick said in a tone so bland she stiffened.

Curtly she told him, "Of course it didn't."

He was watching her with a cynical half-smile she found very off-putting. "Do you want to go home?"

Trust him to face the thing she'd been avoiding. "Why do you ask?" That sounded defensive, and she bristled at his cynical half-smile. "I have to go."

"And spend days coping with Gemma's tears and begging for forgiveness?" Without waiting for an answer he went on, "You need a job. I have one that involves plants and will keep you too busy to rake over the situation you'll find at home."

Siena stared at him. "A job?" she said uncertainly. "What?"

"You said you'd like to work with plants. The garden here needs work. My mother adored cottage gardens, but this is not the place for that sort of garden and the plants have never really thrived. I'd like something different, something that fits this place."

"I'm not a gardener," she told him warily.

"I'm not talking about gardening. It needs a makeover—a complete redesign."

He watched her with an infuriatingly dispassionate gaze as she digested that.

Oh—it sounded wonderful—she'd love to do it…

It would also be extremely dangerous.

Before she could lose her head entirely, she hurried into speech. "Nick, that would be a huge job, and one I'm not trained for. I don't even know if I can come up with a decent garden plan, let alone a complete makeover."

"Don't sell yourself short. You did a damned good job on your parents' garden a couple of years ago," he told her calmly. "I have to leave New Zealand in a couple of days' time, but I'll be in touch. Before I give you the go-ahead I'll need plans and written descriptions, and of course after that I'll expect progress reports wherever I am."

His words hit her like a blow to the heart. He was certainly making sure she understood he didn't plan to be around much. Even so, she should say no and run like crazy as far from Nick as she could.

A clean cut is less painful in the long run, she reminded herself.

But, oh, how she wanted to do it! Why on earth had he asked her…?

A cruel thought struck her. Before she could

think, she asked bluntly, "Is this job a pay-off? As in, thanks for the sex and don't expect anything more?"

Her voice trailed away when Nick's cold gaze bored into her, setting off foreboding and an acute sense of dislocation.

His face hardening into a cold mask, he surveyed her burning cheeks and the mutinous lift of her jaw, and drawled, "You have a very odd idea of my character if you think I pay off ex-lovers." After a taut moment he went on, "And, in the interests of accuracy, I believe that's usually jewellery—something vulgar and glittering and easy to resell."

"Nick—"

"Before you come up with another insult," he interrupted caustically, "I'm *not* doing this because your father helped me at a time when I needed him."

Siena bit her lip. "I'm sorry," she muttered, and yielded to temptation. "It sounds wonderful, and I'd love to give it a go. How about if I work out a plan? That should show me if I can do it. If you don't like it, I'll give you the names of several very good landscape architects who'd make an excellent job of it."

"It's a deal." He held out his hand.

After a moment Siena extended hers. There was nothing sensual about his brisk handshake or his unsmiling look, but Siena felt the impact down to her toes.

With a saturnine smile he said, "And, to stop the remorseful pair from plaguing you with too much angst, I suggest you stay here. If you really feel like being magnanimous tell them we're lovers. I imagine they'll be very grateful and eager to believe you. Grovelling is hard on the self-esteem, and Gemma at least will have an uneasy conscience."

Anger was good. It beat grief any time. Siena bit back hot words and said sweetly, "You're so thoughtful. I might just do that." After a large gulp of coffee she said into the intimidating silence, "In fact, it's a brilliant idea. Am I likely to be contacted by paparazzi, or anybody who feels they might have a prior claim on you?"

At first Nick's expression didn't alter, apart from a slight narrowing of his eyes, but she felt a chill. Her brain went into meltdown.

"No. And stop trying to make me angry."

She could read nothing from the compelling features, nothing in the burnished green of his eyes. His detached tone and disciplined expression sent a shiver scudding down her spine.

"But it's rather fun." She'd intended to say more, but the cool glint in Nick's eyes silenced her.

"Finish your toast."

To her surprise she found herself obeying as he began to tell her what he wanted for the garden.

After a couple of minutes she scrambled to her feet. "I need to make notes. I won't be a moment."

When she got back with her notebook she noticed a fresh slice of toast. Touched, she said, "Thanks."

"Eat it," he commanded, and refused to go ahead until she had.

Scribbling busily, Siena was acutely aware of the sun's blue sheen on his black head, the way the golden light caressed the arrogant angles and planes of his face, and the subtle quickening deep inside her body at his powerful male presence.

Succinctly he described the sort of garden he wanted, finishing, "And you'd better make sure there's a fence—preferably discreet—around the cliff-top."

Siena hoped he assumed the colour in her skin came from the caress of the sun. Her heart twisted painfully, but she was rather proud of her level voice. "It's probably wise. Do you have a time and a price in mind for this? It's not going to be cheap, and it will take some time."

"We can work out the price after I've seen what you come up with," he said. "As for time—I imagine it will take some months, depending on how much building is involved."

"Why me?" she asked directly. "You could get someone with an established reputation. Trust me, landscape architects all over the South Pacific would fight for a commission like this."

"I don't want landscape architects from all over the South Pacific."

"But you don't know that I can do it," she said with blunt honesty, then scrambled to her feet. "Look, the more we talk about it, the more I realise it would be impossible."

His fingers around her wrist shackled her in place; they rested there loosely, with no hint of a threat, but she felt the touch in every cell of her body.

"Sit down," he said quietly.

Siena stared at him, met a gaze that was steady and determined. Uncomfortably she sank back into her chair.

Immediately releasing her, Nick said, "There's no need to lose your courage now."

She bristled. "Lose my courage?"

"That's what you're doing—suffering a crisis of confidence. And, quite frankly, it doesn't sit well with you."

She tilted her chin against his hooded scrutiny. "I—well, I don't want to stuff up," she said lamely, because she *was* being a coward.

She'd loved making over her parents' garden, and was proud of what she'd achieved there. A week ago she'd have fought for this chance, yet now she was using her fear of being hurt to avoid it.

Surely falling in love with Nick hadn't drained her courage away? OK, so she'd be in fairly constant contact, but it would be email—hardly personal. He didn't visit New Zealand more than a couple of times a year, so he probably wouldn't come back until well after the garden was finished.

And by then she might have freed herself from his dark enchantment.

He said, "I'm quite confident you won't allow yourself to fail." Again she felt the full effect of a penetrating survey. Without changing tone he said, "And as you're going to be supervising it would be better if you lived here for the duration."

"All right," she said, adding with a twisted smile, "Nick, you're being very kind. Thank you."

"I'm not particularly kind, so spare me the thanks," he said abruptly. "The arrangement suits me. Tell me, are you happy for Gemma to marry Worth?"

Siena blinked. Odd that only a few days ago she'd been utterly sure she loved Adrian, yet now she could talk about him without feeling anything more than a faint regret. She knew why too, even though she didn't want to accept it. Nick had always been lodged in her heart, and now he'd taken it over completely.

"I don't know," she said truthfully. "What I don't want is for Gemma to blame herself for what's happened. Knowing her, she'll feel guilty all her life. And she's quite capable of turning Adrian down because she's terrified it will wreck my life. It won't."

Nick seemed to be thinking deeply, his unreadable gaze fixed on her face. Finally, when she was getting twitchy, he said, "Your loyalty does you credit." His beautiful mouth curled slightly. "Even though I find it somewhat ironic in the circumstances." He didn't press the issue, continuing smoothly, "How will your parents feel about this abrupt change in everyone's circumstances?"

Heat skimmed her cheeks. "They'll accept it."

"And when we part?"

His laconic query crushed a fragile and foolish hope. With a smile she hoped reached her eyes, Siena said brightly, "I'll make sure they understand it was a mutual decision, not just yours."

His black eyebrows drew together for a second, then the incipient frown smoothed out. "That should cover all bases."

The hint of satire in his words made her look up sharply, but he met her startled gaze with a bland expression.

"I'll have a contract drawn up." This time his tone was all business. "Get a lawyer to go over it with you. In the meantime, we'd better go and collect some clothes from your parents' house."

CHAPTER TEN

As she deposited the cutlery from the terrace table into the dishwasher, Siena said, "I need to give Adrian back his ring." The sooner, the better.

"Courier it to him." Nick's tone gave her no option.

Coolly she returned, "It will be more final if I actually hand it back to him."

"Why?"

With a crooked smile she admitted, "I suppose I want to tell him a few home truths."

"It won't be worth it," Nick said levelly. "If you expect him to be sorry, you'll be disappointed."

"How do you know that?" she demanded.

"Because presumably right now he feels that in Gemma he's found the one true love of his life. What's to be sorry for? You're probably filed under the heading of 'Collateral Damage'."

Siena winced, but had to accept the cynical truth in his words. "Just because he cancelled our engagement by email doesn't mean I have to be as rude. I'm going to give it back personally."

Nick was watching her with half-closed eyes. She could read nothing in his expression.

"Surely that could convince your sister you're still in love with him?"

Siena stared at him, then said slowly, "It shouldn't, but in the state she's in it could, I suppose. I'll just have to make sure she believes our story."

"Give it to me. I'll see that he gets it."

"No, I'll do it." It was ridiculous, but she didn't want Nick to have anything to do with Adrian.

She met his eyes boldly, quelling an odd qualm when he frowned.

However, he left it at that, but when she turned to leave the kitchen he said laconically, "And before we go we'd better make up some story so the details match."

Heat swept up through Siena's skin. Bracing herself, she said brightly, "If anyone asks I'll tell them we met again in London, fell for each other, and that I'm wildly in love with you."

Nick's smile was hardened by a tinge of mockery. "So are we planning a wedding?"

"No!" she blurted, before she had a chance to think.

With a tinge of sarcasm he said, "That reaction is not going to convince anyone that we're conducting a passionate affair. Perhaps you could blush delicately and turn away and say that it's too early yet for such plans."

Siena blinked at his unexpectedly assessing survey. Before she could answer he went on, "Don't bother about it now. I'm sure we can come up with something suitably romantic before we get there."

"*We?* Nick, you don't have to drive me."

"You're going to need me around—at least occasionally—to reinforce the fact that you're violently in love with me," he pointed out smoothly. "And as you don't have a car it will take you all morning to get there by public transport."

Of course he knew she didn't want to spend

money on a taxi across the harbour bridge. Cornered, she snapped, "I hope you're not thinking of coming in with me."

"Not unless you want me to," he said, in a detached voice that probably indicated boredom.

She shook her head, then pushed the dislodged black curls back from her cheeks and met his scrutiny with a rueful smile. "Last night it seemed fairly straightforward," she confessed. "Go back home, reassure Gemma, give Adrian back his ring with a few well-chosen but dignified words, then find a new job and a new place to live. Why is real life a lot more complicated?"

"That's what happens when you start weaving tangled webs." At her bemused glance he quoted, "*'Oh, what a tangled web we weave, when first we practise to deceive.'* Sir Walter Scott is outdated now, but he was a wise man. And if you inveigle other people into your schemes you must expect complications."

"It was not *my* scheme," she objected warily, fighting a swift charge of excitement at the way he was looking at her. "And I don't even know what *inveigle* means."

"I think you do. It means to entice."

Her gaze was caught in the heady snare of his. Adrenalin rushed through her, setting off tiny flickering brushfires of sensation.

"Or seduce." His voice thickened, and with a hand on her shoulder he turned her slightly so that a gentle tug propelled her into his arms. "And, although you probably didn't intend to entice or seduce me, it's very apt," he murmured against her mouth, just before he crushed it beneath his.

The kiss was deep and ravaging, sending arousal pulsing through her. Every thought was swamped by desire so intense Siena's knees buckled under its force.

Nick lifted his head, green eyes smoky with hunger, and then he smiled, stooped and picked her up, heading towards the open door of the sitting room.

On the way across to the sofa she said in a shaken voice, "I get the feeling that carrying me around fulfils some macho power urge you have."

"It certainly makes me feel very, very good," he responded, and lowered himself, long legs stretched the length of the cushions.

He was just as aroused as she was. Her body sprang to life at the familiar faint scent of him, the stripped, intent look in his hooded eyes. Lost to everything but the urgency of her need for him, she traced his beautiful mouth with kisses, butterfly caresses that shortened her breath.

Nick groaned and his hands came down onto her hips, holding her in such intimate juxtaposition she felt the flexion of every sinew and muscle. An answering sound forced its way from her throat as she thrust against him.

Until she remembered what lay ahead of her.

Not now, she thought dazedly when his lips lingered on the hollow of her throat. Little shudders of delight ran through her, fogging her brain with pleasure.

But the intrusive thoughts pushed themselves forward, nagging, refusing to go away.

She lifted her head and said in an anguished voice, "Gemma. And Adrian..."

Narrow-eyed, his voice raw, Nick consigned them to hell directly and without elaboration.

"No," she said, trying hard to smile. "Nick, this is not a good idea right now. I need to be able to think, and I can't do that with a…a passion-dazzled mind."

And a body that wanted nothing more than to surrender to this tantalising, reckless hunger for him.

Nick frowned, but almost immediately his arms dropped. "Passion-dazzled?"

Crimson-faced, she scrambled off, almost stumbling in her eagerness to get away before she did something stupid like kiss him again…

To be on the safe side she strode across the room to stare out of the window. Trees dipped and swayed, flowers were blobs of colour that danced in front of her eyes, but nothing banished the image of Nick magnificently sprawled along the sofa.

"Passion-dazzled," he repeated thoughtfully.

Siena's skin burned even more hotly. Clearly it took no effort for him to quell his hunger.

He said, "I like that very much. I'd like it even more if you hadn't stopped, but you're right."

Contradicting every sensible resolution, she wished he'd ignored her words, taken for himself what they both wanted so much.

She firmed lips that ached for more of his kisses. "I just want to get rid of everything that's hanging over me."

"I can understand that."

Siena turned, her heart bumping unevenly when she saw him fastening the buttons of his shirt. She didn't remember undoing it, but her fingertips thrilled at the memory of his hot skin, fascinatingly textured by the fine pattern of hair across his chest.

She swallowed, but he said, "A clean cut is always the least painful. And it heals better."

Her stomach dropped, and for a far-too-vivid moment she imagined the moment when he would calmly and finally cut free of her.

"Having second thoughts?" he asked, his tone neutral.

Siena shook her head. Whatever happened with

Nick, there could be no going back. Adrian no longer had a place in her heart.

"Far from it," she said crisply. "Let's go."

Gemma was definitely home; the windows had been opened in their parents' house.

Nick stopped the car outside, got out and opened the door for Siena to get out. He looked down at her, his gaze searching. "All right?"

"I'm fine," she said crisply, ignoring the butterflies beneath her ribs.

He bent his head and before she could object he kissed her again—the sort of kiss, she thought dazedly when she emerged from it, that should be kept for very private moments.

"Just in case anyone's watching," he said coolly when she glowered at him.

"There's a good café just around the corner," she said, indicating the top of the street with a jerk of her chin. "I'll meet you there, shall I?"

"I'll wait." He leaned back against the car, big and lithe and magnificent, and clearly determined to stay.

Ruffled by that kiss, she protested, "It's not necessary. You might as well be drinking coffee—"

"Get it over and done with," he said, nodding to two elderly ladies who looked as though they could be making their way home from church.

Both beamed at him, then transferred their smiles—knowledgeably conspiratorial this time—to her.

Warmed, she thought, *If only...*

Because she had to accept the truth. Their supposed affair would end like his previous ones, with no regrets on Nick's part.

She couldn't let that matter now.

Setting her shoulders, she walked up the concrete path, clattered across the wooden verandah and rang the bell, feeling as though Nick had branded her with his kisses.

Gemma opened the door and burst into tears.

"Oh, Gem, don't," Siena said in an anguished voice, and hugged her.

But Gemma couldn't stop; it took Siena almost half an hour before she could make her sister understand that she wasn't shattered, that her heart was otherwise engaged.

She'd packed most of her clothes before Gemma stopped weeping and gasped, "Nick? *Our* Nick?"

Siena said on a sigh, "How on earth you can indulge in a solid half-hour of sobbing and still look gorgeous, I don't know. It's so unfair."

Mopping up, Gemma dismissed this with a wave of her hand. "I'm—actually, I'm not s-surprised. I always knew you had a thing for him. What happened? When did you know it was Nick?"

"When I saw him across the restaurant in London with a gorgeous chilly blonde," Siena told her.

Why on earth hadn't she understood then that the jolt of recognition had spun her world right off its axis? Watching him stride through the hotel restaurant as though he owned the universe had rearranged her life, transforming her into a woman ready to dare dangerously, desperately, even while she accepted there was almost certainly no future for her in a relationship with him.

"Are you *sure*?" Gemma asked worriedly. "*Absolutely* sure Nick is the man for you?"

"Certain," Siena said, with such conviction that Gemma relaxed—although she still looked puzzled, as though she couldn't believe that anyone like Nick could love Siena.

But all she said was, "Where is he now?"

"Out in the car, I assume." Siena got them both a glass of water and said wryly, "No, I see him coming up the path as I speak." Dismay racked her. "With Adrian."

What followed, she thought mordantly in the car afterwards, was like a scene from a French farce. The two men didn't shake hands, and although Nick was polite there was no mistaking the chill in his attitude. Adrian looked somehow smaller, his handsome face almost sullen.

And all it would take was one word for Gemma to start crying again.

Fortunately it didn't last long. Without saying anything Siena handed over to Adrian the small parcel that was her engagement ring. He looked at it as though she'd delivered a snake, and Gemma gave another gulp of dismay, but thank heavens neither said anything.

Within minutes Nick manoeuvred them out of the house and into the car, where Siena sat silently, odd scraps of disconnected thoughts tumbling endlessly though her mind.

After a few minutes Nick said, "What's your problem now?"

Siena tried hard to sound her usual self. "How can you tell when I'm worrying?"

"It's not only women who can read body language," he said dryly. "And stop evading—you do it badly."

She shrugged. "It's not exactly a problem," she said thoughtfully. "It's just that Gemma doesn't seem to know exactly how Adrian feels about her."

Nick sent her an imperious glance. "She probably feels a certain delicacy in confiding to you about him. Keep out of it," he advised with tough pragmatism. "She's a big girl now—she's stolen the man you planned to marry, so she has to live with the consequences. Even as kids you used to rescue her. It's time she learned to run her own life."

Siena had to admit the truth of his astringent view of the situation. She glanced out of the window, and realised they weren't heading for the harbour bridge. "Where are we going?"

"I want to check out my yacht—it's just finished a refit."

Relieved he didn't want to discuss the final painful scene she said, "I didn't know you had a yacht."

"Not your sort," he said dryly.

"You mean a motor yacht? No sails?"

"No sails," he agreed. "While you were in talking to Gemma I got a call from a friend who's been holidaying in Australia. He's decided to see a bit of Northland's coastline, so he's chartering the yacht for a week. I want to speak to the skipper and have a look at the way it's been refitted."

Siena looked sideways, allowing her gaze to linger on the lines and angles of his profile. "I suppose your friend is travelling in a private jet?"

His mouth curved. "Yes. Why?"

"I feel as though I've fallen down a rabbit hole like Alice." She asked suddenly, "How long did it take you to get used to all this stuff—the yacht, the houses, everything?"

"The yacht I bought for my mother," he said. "As for the others—well, I told you the plane's to deliver me in good shape when I need to be on top of a situation. Both yacht and plane get chartered when I'm not using them. I'm not fond of staying in hotels. I'd be a lying fool if I said I don't enjoy the good things I can buy, but I've always known that people are what matter."

Although he hadn't directly answered her question, she felt she'd learned something more about him. He was so difficult to understand, only revealing tiny glimpses of the complex man beneath the sophisticated exterior.

Nick's yacht was moored where the city met the harbour, at a huge marina almost beneath the harbour bridge. Siena got out of the car and went up the gangway, scrupulously keeping her eyes ahead.

Nick had such presence, even in a T-shirt echoing the dense colour of his eyes and a pair of casual trousers that clung to narrow hips and long legs. Siena's stomach tightened, and an intoxicating pleasure shocked her with its swift intensity.

Nick glanced down, caught the absorbed interest in her expression. He did his best to ignore the rapid charged lust that blazed into life whenever he saw her—or even thought of her.

He had no idea what she was thinking, or how she really felt. Not that it mattered. He had her where he wanted her.

The captain came down to meet him. Nick introduced them, curbing a sudden ignoble tension when he noticed the hastily concealed appreciation in the other man's eyes.

"Phil and I need to discuss a few things, but I shouldn't be long," he told Siena. He could have got one of the crew to show her over the vessel, but he was reserving that for himself. "Have a drink here on the sundeck, and when we've finished I'll take you around the yacht."

When he came back she was chatting to the

stewardess, drink forgotten, her curls blowing free in the salt-smelling breeze.

They looked up, and an animated Siena informed him, "Libby and I went to school together and we've been catching up."

With resigned eyes she watched the ex-head girl of her grammar school go a little pink when Nick's lazy green eyes raked her face. Startled by the unwarranted jealousy that stabbed through her, Siena had to stop herself from moving uncomfortably, because she had no right to feel any sort of possessiveness.

Libby excused herself, and Nick asked, "Finished your drink?"

Siena caught sight of the neglected glass. "I didn't even start it."

"Sit down and drink up. There's no need to hurry," he said.

The smile that accompanied his words was a masterpiece; as well as lazy amusement it revealed a potent awareness that sent yet more excitement sizzling from the crown of her head to the ends of her toes.

Stop that right now, she commanded her way-ward body, and concentrated on draining the glass.

To get through this charade without ending in deep trouble she had to keep her head, and sighing over Nick's smile was not going to help her do that.

So she firmed her mouth and said the first thing that came into her mind. "I'm impressed."

"I wonder why I got the idea that you weren't?"

"Come on, who wouldn't be impressed by all this marine glamour?"

"You don't have to pretend—you used to be very contemptuous of motor yachts. I recall you telling me once that true sailing meant you had to have actual sails. Anything else was just boating."

Strangely warmed that he remembered, she produced an elaborate sigh. "I do wish you wouldn't keep reminding me of my brattish, snippy phase. And I'm impressed because you chose a motor yacht that's clean-lined and sturdy. She looks as though she'll be kind in any sea."

"She is." Hot, bright sunlight highlighted his angular features. "I know sailing yachts are far more sexy, but my mother was alive when I bought this for her, and she needed a comfortable vessel."

"And the yacht is named after her?" From the wharf she'd noted the words *Laura Blaine* on the stern.

"Yes. She grew up on a Pacific trading vessel in the Islands. She loved sailing, but by the time I commissioned this she'd developed rheumatoid arthritis. She was barely able to hold the bottle of champagne to christen her, but she relished the chance to explore the Gulf."

Siena looked up to meet his direct, almost speculative gaze, and her stomach contracted in a spasm of tight pleasure. *I want you—now,* she thought urgently, hoping to heaven it didn't show in her face.

Amused, he said, "I did actually have a mother. In fact, you met her fairly regularly."

"It never occurred to me you'd hatched from a pod," she said smartly, "and of course I remember her. I liked her a lot. She must have had a romantic childhood, yet I bet launching the *Laura Blaine* was one of the high points of her life."

"And?" he said.

"And what?"

"What else was going through your mind?"

She blushed hotly, cursing her betraying skin when his scrutiny sharpened. Hastily assembling her thoughts, she said, "Nothing important. Just that although the *Laura Blaine* is lovely there's something about actually being under canvas that no motor yacht can match."

"My mother would have agreed," he told her. "Her father was owner and skipper of one of the last of the sailing traders, and she loved the life."

"It must have been a wrench to give it up and come ashore."

Something darkened his gaze, sending a chill through her. Then it vanished and he said non-committally, "Yes."

Her pleasure was strengthened by a deeper and more elemental emotion. When her eyes met his she recalled the feel of his mouth on hers, on the soft skin of her breasts, girdling her waist with a chain of kisses...

A shiver, torridly sensuous, as though every nerve had been stroked with a feather, swept across her skin. She turned away so he couldn't see her face.

What did he expect of her now? He hadn't touched her since that openly possessive kiss in front of her parents' house, and she wanted—craved—his arms around her with a fierceness that worried her.

But he stayed aloof while he showed her around the yacht. Like his house in London, it had been decorated by a professional, yet somehow it echoed the personality of its owner.

"I like it," she said as he showed her the master stateroom. She glanced up at him, then away again. "It looks superbly comfortable, and practical too—perfect for a yacht."

The cabin was dominated by a very large bed. Hastily Siena's gaze skidded past it to thoroughly approve of the fully stocked bookshelves and the sofa. A lush green plant in a pot brought freshness, and on one wall an abstract oil somehow conveyed the mood of a serene sea under starlight.

Nick indicated a door. "You might want to check out the bathroom." He grinned at her. "Yes, I know it's called the head, but because I often have guests who are not sailors I've slipped into the habit of calling it the bathroom. I'll meet you up on deck."

Once inside the bathroom she turned, wrinkling her nose at the multitude of reflections of herself from the mirrored walls.

I do wish my hair would behave. She washed her hands and pushed an errant curl back from her cheek. The reflections joined her in an elaborate sigh.

Ah, well, she had long ago accepted that not only did she barely make five feet four, but she also possessed hips and breasts, unlike her mother and her sister. One of her early boyfriends had called her a pocket Venus, which had been flattering—until he'd set eyes on Gemma and immediately tried to transfer his allegiance.

"It's a wonder I don't have a complex," she told her reflections, who all grinned somewhat evilly with her.

Then she drew in another deep breath and set her jaw.

Clearly insanity beckoned; only the weird held conversations with themselves.

But a bubble of excitement gave a glitter to her smile that it had never had before, and the anticipation she'd been feeling since Nick had suggested they pretend to be lovers sharpened into something keener and more potent.

That kiss made it seem as though he intended it to be a real relationship, not one in name only...

It was just as well she refused to hope, because back on deck when he said, "Time to go," his aloof tone set an immediate barrier between them.

They drove back to his house almost without speaking. Once there, Nick said, "I've work to do, which will take me at least an hour. What would you like to do? Swim?" He nodded at the infinity pool that seemed to merge with the sea on the horizon.

Several brisk laps of the pool would surely douse the longing that ached through her.

She said, "Yes, that would be great—oh, *bother*."

"What?"

"I don't have any togs with me," she said, dismayed. "I knew I wouldn't be swimming in England, so I didn't take them with me, and although I collected some gear from home just now I didn't think of togs."

Negligently he said, "Swim in whatever you like. The pool isn't overlooked by any other property, so you'll be perfectly safe."

Feeling rebuffed, Siena watched him walk away, all long, smoothly co-ordinated panther strides. Uncontrollable memories of the night they'd spent together in Hong Kong surged up from her wilful unconscious; she swallowed, took a couple of deep breaths, and switched her gaze to the water lapping in the pool.

She needed a swim desperately. It might cool

her head—and the other parts of her body that were uncomfortably hot, as though Nick's presence had set off a chain reaction of tiny electrical shocks.

And it looked hugely inviting out there—the shimmering blue pool surrounded by borders of lush tropical greenery and vivid blooms reflected back like lamps under the water. There was both a shady terrace and one for sun-lovers, furnished with elegantly comfortable recliners, several of them wide enough to take a couple.

He had the complete ensemble—the pool for burning off lust, she thought with a twist of excitement in the pit of her stomach, or recliners for surrendering to it.

Had he made love to anyone here?

No, she did not want to know the answer to that one—unless it was a negative. Even then, it was none of her business. But it took another deep breath and the very firm squelching of a pang of jealousy before she got to her feet.

But neither the water nor a bout of fierce swimming cooled her emotions. Swimming in bra and pants wasn't exactly comfortable, but it was better than lounging in the sun and mulling over things she was never going to ask Nick. Better still, it was a way of exhausting herself; surely physical effort would eventually quench the smouldering desire that ate away at her self-control, at her sense of herself?

Questions buzzed through her mind like angry bees. What did Nick intend? She still didn't know, and he wasn't giving anything away. Was he regretting the passion they'd shared? The long, maddened hours spent making love?

But there was one question she'd kept closeted in some dark recess of her brain. Now, at what she felt was a turning point in her life, she forced herself to face it.

Why had he made love to her so tenderly when she was nineteen, and then left her?

Had he been bored, or embarrassed by her inexperience?

And why hadn't she asked him when they'd met again? Shame? Anger? Bewilderment? No, she admitted, stroking more slowly now, it had been fear.

She'd been afraid to ask because whatever answer he gave would hurt too much.

She wished now she'd asked her father more about Nick's childhood, and then grimaced, because of course her father wouldn't have told her.

If anyone were to, it would have to be Nick, and why should he? It was clearly still something he didn't want to talk about.

In the end she scolded herself for being foolishly obsessive, and concentrated with all her will on her breathing, keeping her thoughts at bay by recounting her swimming coach's instructions.

Until she lifted her streaming face from the water and saw Nick, already in the pool. Startled and suddenly shy, she sank beneath the water.

Seconds later a jerk on her arm opened her eyes wide as she shot to the surface, Nick's hand locked almost painfully around her wrist.

"Are you all right?" His expression grim, he tipped her head back and examined her face. "What the hell were you doing?"

"Hiding," she said succinctly, colour burning along her cheekbones.

He let his eyes drop, and something kindled in them, banishing the last of his concern. Loosening his grip, he asked quietly, "Why?"

"I didn't expect to see you here."

His brows drew together. "I live here, remember? And don't tell me you're afraid of me, because I won't believe you."

Of course she wasn't afraid of him; she was afraid of what her aching, vulnerable heart might lead her to say…to do…

"It can't be an hour since I got in the pool," she accused, defiantly refusing to let her gaze linger on his broad, bronzed shoulders and chest.

"I cut things short. I also said I wouldn't look, so you didn't need to sink to the bottom." The pause that followed gave his next words extra emphasis. "And you may be noticing that, apart from once, I've very nobly—and with great difficulty—refrained from anything more than one glance, just to reassure myself you were still breathing."

Colour burned through her skin, but before she could say anything, he went on with an edge to his tone, "Although why are you worrying? Not only have I seen every inch of your delectable body, I've kissed almost all of that exquisite skin. At the time, you didn't seem to mind."

CHAPTER ELEVEN

Siena's eyes widened and colour flooded her skin as she searched in vain for some snappy come-back.

Nick's laugh came from deep in his throat. "I didn't know you could blush all over."

"You said you wouldn't look!" she accused, hot-cheeked and agitated.

"I'm only human. It's like watching a white rosebud turn pink. Did you put sunscreen on?"

The abrupt shift from darkly sensual appreciation sent an odd little shiver though her. "Of course I did," she muttered.

He turned her around and said, "But you can't reach the centre of your back. I'll get it."

Siena watched him take two strokes to the side of the pool and haul himself out. Although he was wearing togs, they revealed far more than they hid as water streamed in sheets of silver light over a body honed and muscular, sleek yet powerful.

A disturbing mixture of excitement and apprehension churned beneath her ribs, as though she was about to take the biggest decision she'd ever made—a huge step into an unknown, exhilarating future, shadowed by the prospect of shattering pain.

But there would be no disillusion. Nick made no vows. It would be an honest relationship—on his part, she admitted.

Because she didn't dare tell him she loved him. She suspected that if she did he'd close her out without even thinking about it.

Nick turned, catching her eyes on him. He looked quizzical, and there was an undertone she couldn't place when he said, "What big eyes you have."

"You know the answer to that one," she said without thinking. *All the better to see you with...*

His mouth hardened, then relaxed into a smile that promised everything she wanted, the satisfaction of all her desires—except the most important.

But love had no place here.

He said, "You need to dry your back before I put this on."

"Yes," she said, recklessly casting the dice.

Nick stooped and took her outstretched hands, pulling her easily out of the water. She glanced down and realised her bra was totally transparent, but even as colour surged back up he turned her away.

When his hands came to rest on her shoulders she shivered deliciously.

His grip loosened a fraction. "Cold?" he asked softly.

She licked her lips, then said on the same quiet note, "No."

One finger eased beneath the catch of her bra. "Good. Because it would make things much easier if I took this off."

Beneath the even, humorous tone of his voice she heard a raw note of authentic passion.

And everything came right in her world. She

relinquished every last scruple, because this was what she wanted. If she let her fears and concerns steer her away from Nick she'd always regret it.

So she'd follow her heart.

She looked over her shoulder, the sensuous flutter at the base of her spine burning into a conflagration when she met his unfathomable green gaze.

A delicious languor melted her bones and she had to swallow and clear her throat before she could say huskily, "All right, then. Take it off."

It was free in an instant, falling loosely around her. She dragged in a deep breath, her breasts rising and falling sharply at a light kiss on one shoulder. It lasted only a second, and desperate to feel his arms around her she began to swivel, only to squeak when his teeth grazed the place he'd just kissed.

"Siena?"

"Yes." Nerves singing, she turned to look up at him.

His face angular and tightly controlled, he seemed to be waiting. Siena lifted her hand and placed the sensitive palm in the middle of his chest, where his heart was thudding heavily.

Breathy and sensuous, her voice startled her when she said, "You are magnificent."

His gaze fell to her breasts. "So are you. Exquisite in every way."

The impact of his scrutiny was like a caress, heating her skin, bringing the tight little tips of her breasts to full alert.

"Are you sure, Siena?"

She gestured vaguely. "Can't you see?"

Adrenalin burned through her at the flare of dark fire in his eyes.

But he didn't move. In a voice that came close to being guttural, he said, "I've been wanting this since Hong Kong."

"So have I."

His cheek creased in a smile that held wry amusement. "Idiots, both of us—although the wait was necessary."

Siena nodded, hope stirring in the depths of her heart. He had understood feelings she barely recognised, the need to put her own stamp on the end of one relationship before she could give herself fully to another.

He said smoothly, "And if I carry you across to the lounger over there—" he was sweeping her into his arms as he spoke, making her squeak again and clutch his shoulders "—that white skin of yours will be protected from the sun, and the sunscreen can wait…"

Water slicked their skin, somehow linking them, so that when he deposited her on the broad length of one of the big recliners she felt abandoned—a feeling abruptly terminated when Nick came down beside her, his arms closing around her in a grip that didn't feel as though he'd ever let go.

A fierce delight surged through her and her bra dropped unheeded to the ground. Here—in Nick's arms—was the only place she ever wanted to be.

For long seconds they lay together, heart against heart, their pulses slowly synchronising until wonderingly she could hear and feel only one—a beat that increased yet again when he tilted her head back and looked into her eyes.

Siena's breath came quickly through her parted lips. Nick's face was drawn into a mask of passion, yet his mouth on hers was almost gentle, as though afraid of hurting her.

Lost to desire, Siena closed her eyes and surrendered to the hunger uncoiling through her in a surge of hot, wildly sweet passion.

When he lifted his head she smiled, letting the air out of her lungs in a lingering sigh. Her lashes quivered against her cheeks; she didn't look at him in case her eyes gave away her new-found love.

"Siena?"

Why did some lucky men have the sort of voice that made women's toes curl? Deep and cool and spine-tingling... Desire—insistent, compelling—throbbed through her.

"Siena, look at me."

She resisted for a few seconds longer before dragging in a fortifying breath and obeying him. "You keep saying that."

"It's so I can make some attempt to find out what you're thinking." Nick's eyes were penetrating. "How did it feel to see Adrian Worth this morning?"

A chill ran through her. In the strong sanctuary of his arms her mindless surrender to passion would temporarily banish any thought of a future without Nick—would overwhelm everything beyond the hunger that ached through her in a surge of painful longing.

But she could feel the strength of his determination, a force she had no power to shatter. And she understood it was important to say what she had to say.

"Strange," she told him unevenly. "Like looking at the old photos in my parents' albums and realising how different I was then, how much I've changed since they were taken. How everything has changed."

Adrian is the faded past, she wanted to say; *you are the full-colour present.*

But she couldn't. She didn't dare. Soon she might be an old photograph in Nick's album, and she was just learning that without him there would be no more colour, no true pleasure in life. Her heart quailed.

"What is it?" Nick asked abruptly, his face intent, almost predatory. "What's the matter?"

"Nothing," she said steadily. No matter how this ended, she'd go on, and she'd find satisfaction in her existence.

Loving Nick had changed her fundamentally. She had quite literally become a different woman from the one who'd thought she loved before. Against what she felt for Nick that illusory love had been weak and temporary—a practice run rather than the real thing.

She looked up into half-closed eyes, intent and glittering. Quietly she said, "Nothing's the matter. Whatever we had wasn't strong enough to meet any challenges. We're not the same people we were when we got engaged, and I don't love him any more. It's gone, over, finished."

"And how do you feel about that?" Nick probed relentlessly.

She couldn't lie. "A little regretful, but a little foolish too."

It was all she dared say. Anything more might reveal the true state of her feelings, and Nick wouldn't want to know.

She longed to experience everything she could with Nick, fill her heart with memories, and she wouldn't let her fears about the future stop her from indulging her love in the present.

She'd deal with that future—and Nick's absence from it—when she had to. For this moment, Nick's arms about her—*this* was the present...

Candidly, she said, "You must realise I want you. And I don't expect promises or vows, either. I suspect I'm rather over them right now. Let's just take things as they come, shall we?"

She reached up and pulled his head down and kissed him, boldly signalling her hunger, her body sinuous and tense as she pressed against him. Without hesitation he responded, and her heart sang when he tore his mouth from hers and looked into her eyes.

"No vows," he promised in a low, gravelly growl.

This time their lovemaking was fierce, a wild sharing of rapture that carried Siena beyond everything she'd ever known about herself.

Much later, coming down in Nick's arms from unimaginable ecstasy, she wondered how on earth anyone could endure such rapture and not die of it.

She'd been lost—lost in desire, lost to everything but how much physical delight her body could feel.

She was also lost in love. She loved Nick with everything in her, her emotion strong enough to encompass passion and trust and commitment—a yearning that ached through her with such power that without him her life would be grey and weary and shapeless, an echoing waste of breath.

Could there be any chance of Nick loving her in return?

In a way he already did, she thought painfully. But that kind of love—the *girl-next-door grows up* love—wasn't what she wanted from him. He'd been kind and thoughtful and helpful. He certainly desired her. He was a fantastic lover.

Yet if she hadn't found herself with a problem in London he'd have gone to Hong Kong without her. They'd have said goodbye, gone their separate ways, and she'd have seen him next in some gossip magazine with another exquisite blonde on his arm.

What she wanted from him was her kind of love—the all-in, no-holds-barred sort, a love like her parents' that would grow and change and last a lifetime.

With the solid, heavy thud of his heartbeat in her ears, his arms holding her against his lean body, the scent of their lovemaking so erotically stimulating she could feel her innermost parts stir with longing again, she forced herself to drag in a painful breath.

There was a term for that sort of yearning—crying for the moon. Nick had made no mention of anything but desire.

She couldn't allow such a complete surrender again. She had to be like Nick and protect herself—keep her treacherously crumbling barriers intact, protect herself with all her strength from such an addictive need.

But how?

Those two bleak words told her it was already far too late.

In a rough voice he said, "Asleep?"

"No."

He moved, held her a little away so he could see her face. "When do your parents come home?"

Siena had to think before she could give him the date.

"Just on three weeks from now," he said. "I'll be back by then, but before I leave we'd better get all of your stuff over here."

"Back?" she stammered, completely thrown. "I thought—you said you were going away."

His eyes were cool and hard—no trace of residual passion, she noted, and certainly nothing of love in that keen gaze. "I'm not going to stay away."

"Oh. I thought you—well, you don't normally spend much time in New Zealand."

He frowned. "And I thought we were supposed to be madly in love," he said dryly. "That means fairly close contact. As you're going to be busy with the garden, naturally I'll be based here from now on."

Her heart leapt, but she forced herself to be practical. "I'm assuming this is an invitation to share your house and bed for a while?" she said, as crisply as she could.

His mouth curved. "Bear with me—I've never asked anyone to live with me before."

Siena reined in her racing pulse. "Never?"

"No."

When he left it at that she said primly, "There didn't appear to be any asking involved. I got the distinct impression I was being told—in a roundabout way."

He surveyed her face with an expression she couldn't read. "My PA is going to think you're just what I deserve." He locked his arms around her to pull her hard against him.

The vague wisp of memory concerning that

efficient PA in London, with her children and her househusband, fled from Siena's mind.

In her ear he said harshly, "Siena, not only will staying here make your valiant attempts to smooth things over for your sister and your parents much more likely to succeed, it will give me enormous pleasure to have you close." His voice deepened. "And I can promise you'll enjoy it too."

For as long as it lasts, she thought on a flash of anguish. "Perhaps we should think—" she began, only to have the words stopped by his mouth.

Fleetingly she thought she might have been able to resist if it had been a passionate, hungry kiss. Instead it was sweet and tender, baffling common sense, making only one decision possible.

When he lifted his head, he said roughly, "What's your decision?"

It took all her courage to whisper, "Yes." She cleared her throat and said more boldly, "I'll stay here."

However, he didn't take her surrender at face value. "Was it so hard?"

Hard? It was hell—and heaven. The promise of

a short heaven, with the surety of a long hell. But what could she say? Like a coward, she evaded. "Like you, I haven't ever stayed—lived with anyone. I don't know the protocol."

His eyes narrowed, but to her relief he didn't push. "Then we'll learn together."

Together...

One word, yet it gave her hope, probably spurious, almost certainly doomed. She didn't even know if he could feel anything beyond passion. And she wanted more from him than that tenderly fierce drive to possess.

Hoping she was wrong, she doubted if he'd ever understand the emotion that gripped her now, propelling her into a situation she knew could cause her unbearable pain.

In fact he'd cancel the whole deal if she blurted out that she loved him.

For a moment she was tempted to do just that, but all loving came entwined with the prospect of pain; to refuse its joys because it meant caring too much would be to turn her back on life.

And her impatient heart would never stop nurturing a hope that one day he would look at her and see someone he loved.

"So we will," she said quietly.

His mouth twisted. "Not that we're going to enjoy each other for long this time," he said. "I've just had a message from my PA; I have to go to San Francisco to a meeting. I should be back within the week."

"OK," she said, hiding a bleak pang of dismay with an airy smile. "When do you leave?"

"In an hour."

She managed a laugh. "Then you'd better get packing," she advised, hoping her insouciance rang true.

He didn't want her to come to the airport with him, so they said their farewells at the house. Siena was a little reassured by the fierceness of his embrace.

"I'll start thinking about the garden," she promised.

"Think of *me* occasionally," he commanded coolly, then dropped his arms and turned away.

Of course she thought of him constantly. He

rang every night, and during those talks she felt herself falling ever more in love with him. Although discreet, he made her laugh—and sometimes gasp—with short, occasionally brutal character studies of the people he was dealing with. And she told him about her method of learning about the garden.

"Lots of walking around and staring at things," she said. "And squinting and imagining other things in their place. And sketches and notes."

"Are you enjoying it?"

"Very much." *And missing you...*

"I'll see you soon. Don't work too hard." He paused, then said, "Are you swimming?"

"No," she said, although the pool beckoned her every day. She laughed. "Mum has a thing about swimming alone—I've been brainwashed into thinking it's highly dangerous—almost as bad as going into a paddock with a Jersey bull."

He laughed, but said, "Keep safe."

Siena woke with a start at the sound of her name. *Nick,* she thought, dazed with delight, and scrambled to her feet. Too late, she remembered she wasn't in her bed, and gave a startled yelp as she crash-landed on the wooden floor.

"What the hell—? *Siena!*"

"I'm here," she croaked. She muttered something as she tried to untangle herself from the thin blanket she'd carried down to the summer-house.

He stood in the opening, a dark figure against the soft summer midnight outside. "What the hell are you doing here?" he demanded, crossing the floor in two strides and picking her and the blanket up from the floor. His arms closed tightly around her. "Are you all right?"

"I'm—I'm fine." She struggled upright in his embrace.

He said, "Why are you here?"

"I was hot, so I came down here to sleep…"

"Dear God, I thought—I thought—" He walked across to the sofa and sat down on it, holding her as carefully as though she were the most precious thing on earth to him.

In a voice she'd never heard before he said, "I thought you'd gone."

"Gone?"

"Yes," he said quietly. His chest rose and fell against her. "And I knew something then that I've been fighting for—for ever, it seems."

Siena looked up, able to discern only the contours of his face in the dimness. Anxiety filled her as she scanned the drawn, hard angles of his face.

He said, "I knew then that hard as I've tried—and God knows I've exhausted more energy denying this than I have in achieving anything else—I knew that if you left me I'd never forget you, never stop longing for you."

Unable to believe she'd heard properly, Siena blinked and shook her head to clear it.

Nick's mouth tightened. Still in that strange voice she'd never heard before he said, "Don't you believe me? Then I'll just have to work at convincing you."

Swiftly she said, "I shook my head because everything was jumbled up in it, and for a moment

I thought I was dreaming. I—Nick, I want to believe you—you have no idea how much I want to."

He was silent, then said unevenly, "Well, thank God for that."

She took a deep breath and with desperate courage—or foolhardiness—said shakily, "I'm just—just finding it very difficult. You've not shown—I mean, I knew you wanted me—but that's not—what you're talking about is love."

And held her breath.

Whatever, *knowing* what Nick felt for her had to be better than this horrible no-man's-land she'd been enduring.

He tensed, and the seconds ticked by, and then he said in a taut, driven voice, "Yes. It has to be love."

Her breath sighed out. "It's about time," she told him fiercely. "I've loved you for years and years—"

Nick choked back a laugh, deep and male and hugely satisfied, then said, "You *love* me? Are you sure?"

Siena didn't hesitate. Her heart in her words, she told him, "I've loved you ever since I was old enough to know what love is. I just didn't realise it. I loved you when we made love together that first time—"

He said, "It was the first time for you, wasn't it?"

"Yes," she said simply.

He shook his head and accused, "You let me believe you'd had other experience."

"Would you have made love to me if I hadn't?"

His jaw hardened. "Probably not. Although— how the hell do I know? I wish I'd known."

"I don't think it would have made any difference," she said quietly.

"I must have hurt you so much when I walked out."

"Yes," she said simply.

His arms tightened again. Locked in that fierce grip, Siena knew with a sure, radiant joy that her yearning heart had reached its goal. In Nick's arms she was home.

He said, "So you chose someone safe, someone you didn't love, someone who couldn't hurt you?"

"Yes. Until you charged in like some buccaneer and carried me off to Hong Kong. And I—" She turned her face into his shoulder and corrected herself. "No, *we* made love."

Quietly he said, "And you had an orgasm for the first time."

"It wasn't that—or not just that." She looked up at him, her eyes searching out the hard line of his jaw, the fierce framework that would keep him handsome all his life. "I wondered that too—and accused myself of being shallow, thinking it was too soon to know…" She stopped, then went on more strongly, "But it isn't too soon because I've always loved you. I just had to let myself accept it."

He said with a quiet intensity that removed any last shred of doubt from her mind, "My very dear heart."

He stopped, and she felt his chest lift against her. Incredulously, she realised the hope she'd cherished was springing into full-blown bloom.

And then, at last, he kissed her.

Later, when they'd arrived back at the house, he poured champagne. "To us," he said, handing her a glass. "And to our future."

She laughed up at him, and said, "Shouldn't we be toasting Gemma and Adrian? If it hadn't been for them I wouldn't have gone to Hong Kong with you and we might never have known—might have spent our lives looking for someone."

Nick made a sound remarkably like a snort. "It would have happened," he told her. "I might have been too thick-headed to understand what I felt for you, but I'd have got there in the end."

She smiled a little shakily at him. Before she could say anything he added in an entirely different voice, hard and flat, "I knew I had to do something when I caught sight of that damned ring on your finger."

Siena stared at him, saw the naked truth in his face. "Do something?" she asked uncertainly.

"I felt as though someone had stolen the only thing that mattered to me. It was almost obscene that you should be wearing another man's ring.

The thought of you making love with him made me want to go out and lay waste to the world."

Nick had always been so controlled, so self-reliant, she found it difficult to imagine him capable of such extravagant emotion.

Yet she was convinced. He said tautly, "It also made me afraid."

"Afraid?" she asked, not believing him.

His mouth twisted. "In the house I grew up in it was downright dangerous to show your feelings."

"Your father?" she asked slowly, almost afraid to probe any further.

"Yes. He was a despot."

He walked across to the window and looked outside, yet Siena doubted if he saw anything in the moon-glossed garden. Chilled, rubbing her upper arms nervously, she didn't prompt; she waited, knowing that this was the key to Nick, the reason control was so important to him.

Without turning his head he said, "My father didn't physically abuse my mother, or me, but he used our emotions to control every aspect of our lives. I was his weapon against her; when he was angry with her I was the one who suffered, so she was very careful not to do anything that would make him angry. We never knew what would set him off, so I grew up controlling every outward expression of emotion. By the time my mother left him she was a nervous wreck, which is how he got custody. Then she recovered, I went to live with her, and he committed suicide. His death was a relief to both of us."

Horrified, Siena said, "I understand."

"I hope you don't." A steely note in his words revealed just how much he wasn't telling her. "I asked her once why she'd stayed with him. She said she loved him. And she told me—probably out of misplaced loyalty—that he'd loved me. That's when I decided, I suppose, that love wasn't worth it."

Still in that cool, judicial tone he went on, "Seeing your father with you and Gemma, with your mother, convinced me my *father* was the one at fault—not my mother, not me. But I still didn't understand love. And then five years ago

I came back from overseas and met you again, and you were utterly enchanting and I couldn't resist you."

"And you resented me," she said, almost afraid to say the words she knew had to be spoken.

He turned then. "Not you—never you! I did resent the fact that I couldn't control my feelings for you."

Siena went across and looped her arms around his big frame. He was rigid, as though this explanation of his feelings was costing him far more than she could understand.

After a moment he relaxed, and looked down at her with a lopsided smile. "You were fearless and independent and funny, and I wanted you so desperately it scared the wits out of me. I knew what I should do—leave you alone. It was a huge blow to my self-esteem to find I couldn't. I found myself becoming possessive, and that rang alarm bells. But I still couldn't do the decent thing and walk away. And then we made love, and it was something I'd never expected—a complete giving of myself. I wanted all of you, for ever. So I played the coward."

He paused, then said, as though the words were wrenched from him, "It was hell to be forced to accept that I have enough of my father in me to develop that urge to control."

"I don't believe for a moment that you're anything like your father!" Siena said indignantly. "Clearly there was something very mixed-up in him."

"I was concerned enough to discuss him with a friend—a psychiatrist. He felt my father must have lacked confidence that my mother would stay with him, so he used whatever weapons he had to make sure she couldn't leave. Instead, he drove her into a breakdown. When I went to live with her he had nothing, no way of controlling either of us. So he killed himself."

"Do you blame yourself for that?"

She held her breath until he answered. "I did at first. When she applied for custody I was asked by the social agency which parent I wanted to live with. I told them I wanted to live with my mother. Killing himself might have been a last-ditch attempt to gain sympathy; I don't know. Perhaps he just hoped she'd suffer some sort of remorse for the rest of her life."

"It's a miracle you grew up so—so stable," she said unevenly.

"You can thank my mother and your parents—but mainly your father—for that. He showed me that a man can love without wanting to domi-nate." He looked at her with a naked longing. "That primitive instinct to keep my woman close might be hardwired into me, but I know the link between you and your family will never be broken."

Something tightened around her heart. "You're included too, Nick—you're already part of the family."

She longed to be in his arms, to hold him close, but she sensed that this was not a time for that.

Instead she said, "On your own terms, of course. But when we forge new links the old ones are..." She searched for the right words to explain what she meant, eventually settling on,

"They're not weakened. The new ones might become stronger, but the old ones are still there— like the link between you and your mother when your father had custody."

His smile twisted. "I might have enough of my father in me to periodically try and assert an authority I have no right to claim, but I can control my feelings, and I love you." He stopped, then said unevenly, "I've never said that to anyone else, and I'm glad I waited until I could mean it."

Tears filled her eyes, and he caught her to him, holding her with such gentleness her heart melted.

In a muffled voice she demanded, "What took you so long? You must have guessed that I loved you five years ago."

"I tried to make you hate me. Even in London I couldn't see that you'd ever forgive me for what I did to you."

"Oh," she said, on a long sigh of understanding.

He nodded. "But I think I always hoped. In Hong Kong I discovered that the world was far more vivid and bright, full of delight just because you were with me. And now I know that without you there will be no colour for me, no peace, no satisfaction in my life."

"Exactly," she said quietly, lifting her arms to cup his face. Her fingers tingled against the rough silk that was his beard. "From now on it's us, Nick."

Blue eyes met green, and clung, and this time there was no challenge, nothing but trust.

Yet still Nick didn't kiss her. As though making a vow, his voice very deep and sure, he said, "And, because I'm aware of this tendency to come over all primitive where you're concerned, I won't allow it to wreck our lives. You and your family are close, but I understand your love for them isn't taking anything away from what we— you and I—have. I don't want to own you."

He held her away from him and smiled down at her, his expression open so that she could read the trust and the love there.

"You wouldn't let me, anyway," he said.

They kissed, and with complete faith she surrendered the last bastion of her heart to him, confident he'd keep his word.

"Siena. Darling, wake up."

Siena woke to her husband's quiet voice. Automatically her hand went to her stomach. "Mmm?" she murmured, then gasped as the muscle beneath her palm tightened and a wave of tension gripped her.

"I think it's time," she said when it eased.

"You've been making odd little noises for about half an hour," Nick told her.

The telephone shrilled. He gave a muted laugh and lifted it. "Yes," he said. "I'm taking her to the hospital right away." His gaze lingered on his wife's face as he listened. "OK, I'll do that."

He put the phone down. "Gemma sends her love," he told his wife, scooping her up and setting her on her feet with infinite tenderness. "And I have to let her know as soon as I can after the baby is born."

An hour and a half later he looked down into

the face of the tiny boy in his arms and said thoughtfully, "Next time—if there is a next time—you're going to spend the last week in the nursing home. Both the midwife and obstetrician said the second baby tends to arrive more quickly."

Siena laughed. Waves of tiredness swept over her, but she was filled with exhilaration, the kind of soul-deep happiness she'd almost grown accustomed to in the past couple of years. "There will be a next time," she said confidently. "But not straight away—and this birth was so easy I'm sure I can have our next baby at home."

The baby started to whimper and Nick looked concerned. "Do you think he's afraid?"

"No," she reassured him. "How can he be? You're holding him. You're his father and he already knows your voice."

Nick sat down in the chair beside the bed and held the precious bundle up against his shoulder, competently stroking the tiny back until their son's whimpering stopped.

His father said, "I think he's missing you.

When he gets used to us we'll take him to Hong Kong, shall we? We won't tell him it's the place where we found out we loved each other until he's grown up, but it will always be special to me because of that."

She smiled mistily at him. "I'd love that. It's very special to me too."

A few moments later the door opened, then hastily closed again. Neither new parent heard it; they were too busy kissing—carefully, so as to keep their child in the warm circle of their arms.

* * * * *

Mills & Boon® Large Print

January 2012

THE KANELLIS SCANDAL
Michelle Reid

MONARCH OF THE SANDS
Sharon Kendrick

ONE NIGHT IN THE ORIENT
Robyn Donald

HIS POOR LITTLE RICH GIRL
Melanie Milburne

FROM DAREDEVIL TO DEVOTED DADDY
Barbara McMahon

LITTLE COWGIRL NEEDS A MUM
Patricia Thayer

TO WED A RANCHER
Myrna Mackenzie

THE SECRET PRINCESS
Jessica Hart

Mills & Boon® Large Print
February 2012

THE MOST COVETED PRIZE
Penny Jordan

THE COSTARELLA CONQUEST
Emma Darcy

THE NIGHT THAT CHANGED EVERYTHING
Anne McAllister

CRAVING THE FORBIDDEN
India Grey

HER ITALIAN SOLDIER
Rebecca Winters

THE LONESOME RANCHER
Patricia Thayer

NIKKI AND THE LONE WOLF
Marion Lennox

MARDIE AND THE CITY SURGEON
Marion Lennox